Mystery Without Any Clues

Joseph Albanese

Writers Club Press

San Jose New York Lincoln Shanghai

Mystery Without Any Clues

Writers Club Press
an imprint of iUniverse.com, Inc.

For information address:
iUniverse.com, Inc.
5220 S 16th, Ste. 200
Lincoln, NE 68512
www.iuniverse.com

ISBN: 0-595-13849-7

Printed in the United States of America

Mystery Without Any Clues

To C^2, EZ and TE, Esq. My Ladies. Thanks.

ONE

Boring. That's what life had turned into-one long, boring series of events that seemed never to vary or sway in any direction except the one's that they had followed for years.

Looking out of the apartment window Jeremy Baker stared at the street several stories below and felt the burning, frustrated ends of a fruitless day leading toward a fruitless life.

Coming out from the kitchen, wiping his hands on a small towel with a country motif design stitched onto it, Jeremy's lover-Sheraton Rogers-immediately picked up the tell-tale signs of disharmony.

It was like that. It had always been that way-from their college day meeting up to the present. Sheraton was happy because he wanted to be happy. Jeremy found his shyness and inability to deal with strangers and new situations to lead him into frustration.

After several years together, they had managed to achieve some sense of harmonial balance by accepting the others more endearing qualities while trying their best to ignore the circumventing traits.

"It's the middle of the week," Jeremy said, his hands wrecking havoc with the thin slats of the blinds as he continued to stare out the window. "Work tomorrow. A weekend of grocery shopping and laundry and television. Then what?"

Sheraton was wise enough, and enough in tune with Jeremy's moods, to avoid a direct answer. He usually kept the smile on his clear, midwesternly boyish face by accepting most of Jeremy's semblance's as a creative challenge.

"Why not go out for an hour or so?" he suggested, putting down the towel as an act of his eagerness to do just that.

"On a school night?" Neither of them had been in school for some time. It was work-Sheraton's job at a department store and Jeremy's desk job at a small publishing firm-and little else.

"Yes," Sheraton grinned. He looked so soft in his blonde, fair way that it was difficult for people to determine just how much steel there was deep within him. "Let's go down to Christopher Street and have a drink."

"Just because we live in the Village it doesn't mean we have to bar hop always," Jeremy said.

"All the time? Honey, the last time we went out for a drink I think we had to show proof of our age."

"No fear of that happening now," Jeremy said, suddenly seeing his reflection in the window pane. His hair, dark and bushy, was frosted with a smattering of gray around the temples and-something he found unbearable-mixed in at odd spots throughout his mustache.

"At least it'll be a change from the usual," Sheraton suggested easily. He knew it never paid to push Jeremy into anything.

"Standing in a bar that's dark, smoky and filled with cardboard cut-outs isn't a change-it's degrading."

Passing his thirtieth birthday hadn't sweetened Jeremy. Now, instead of looking ahead, he looked back. Before him he could only see old age and death. Behind him it wasn't much better-a lonesome childhood. A kid raised in the rough part of Manhattan. A sensitive, unimaginative sort of boy who had a weight problem and a constant fear of rejection.

There was a world and a different life out there but he was afraid of it just as he was afraid to admit that it scared him. Sheraton knew and understood all this without talking about it, ever.

"Just a quick beer and then home," Sheraton suggested again. "You never know what might happen."

"We might get mugged or become drunks or both."

"Or," Sheraton thought, "we might have fun."

Turning from the window, Jeremy looked around the small apartment. It was decorated to his taste. An elaborate portion of the small living room was turned over to him for his stereo equipment. A small space, hardly roomy enough for all the peripherals, was allotted to Sheraton for his home computer. The colors were a quirky combination of their favorites-blue for Jeremy and sunshine yellow for Sheraton. Everything about the place seemed impossible but, in the long run, it had merged into an atmosphere that was comfortable and unpressurized.

"One drink," Jeremy said as he slipped his shoes back onto his feet. "One drink and then home again."

"Right," Sheraton said. It was something so ordinary that it shouldn't have even been worthy of a second thought on his part but Sheraton found a small comfort in Jeremy's willingness to go out. Sheraton had nothing against domesticity but he also had nothing against experimental trysts either.

How were either of them to know what was going to happen?

*   *   *

Sheraton was beginning to feel that he was going to introduce a new concept in their lives-having fun. He would have liked to have changed, combed his hair and done several other small incidentals but he didn't. He wouldn't do anything to give Jeremy a chance to back down now.

When the phone rang, they were half way out the door and fumbling between themselves to see who would retrieve his keys first. Sheraton wanted to ignore the phone; Jeremy would ignore the phone but a curiosity-and the gaping door that still wasn't locked-propelled Sheraton into picking up and answering before the fifth ring.

After he hung up, he gave Jeremy a small smile and tried to keep his voice light.

"That was Jazz," he said. "He wants us to meet him. I suggested the bar—"

Jeremy's groan, Sheraton felt, could be heard all the way to the bar.

"Do we have to have Jazz along?"

"Jeremy, it's important to Jazz that he does have friends."

All Jeremy could see was Jazz in his mind-snake hip slim, tousled hair and not too brainy. And a drag queen.

"I suppose it's better than having him up here," Jeremy agreed, not liking the sound of such a statement but too annoyed to retract it.

They walked outside and into the night. The wind was playing a medley of hot and cold. Breezes warmed and cooled so that it gave the night a carefree, lark-like feel to it. Many people casually strolled down the streets on Bleecker and looked into the lit shop windows as they passed by them.

It was when they were looking into a shop with a slightly dirty window and shelves filled with antique toys that Jeremy allowed his guilty feelings to come forward.

"I suppose that what I'm doing right now is prejudice."

Sheraton, not able to tolerate even the sound of the word, tried to soften it while he explained to Jeremy:

"It's not easy for any of us. I would imagine that, for Jazz, to do what he has to do is even harder. We can get by and be easily written off by some as room mates—"

"I always wondered about *The Odd Couple*,"

"—it's not so easy for Jazz. Just as we couldn't deny our true feelings any longer, neither can he."

"But do his true feelings have to involve padded bras and shoes with heels so high that they would have given Joan Crawford a nose bleed?"

Sheraton, as usual, found silence to be his sanest form of defense. Besides, Jeremy apologized-in his fashion-and would accept Jazz when he showed up-also in his fashion, crusty as it may be.

To prolong the inevitable-Jeremy didn't feel very good about standing around in bars-he led the way in a round-about route that circumnavigated the Hudson River. As much as Jeremy complained to Sheraton about the cold, he didn't protest as they stood on the freezing street while the lights from the Jersey Shore twinkled merrily in the distance.

"Most of the bars around here don't like drag," Jeremy said making Sheraton wonder if he were trying to cut short their bar hop even before it began. "Funny when you think of it. They accept whips, leather and motor cycle bikers who practically pull up to the bar area still on their bikes."

"I guess it's still specialized," Sheraton speculated.

"Maybe if the guy's who wanted to do drag would just dress up normally-if a man wearing a dress could ever be thought of as normal-instead of doing a pseudo-Dolly Parton imitation. Over emphasis is bad enough when you have guys running around in leather socks but two pounds of make-up and a wig piled high enough to scrape away another layer of ozone is a bit too much."

"Jazz isn't that bad," Sheraton commented, wondering if Jeremy would recall the day-glo outfit that Jazz had greeted them in the last time they met.

Judging from the look of discomfort, Jeremy was about to remember the dress that he couldn't hide even with the lights off when they heard they're names being called.

"Who can that be?" Jeremy asked, staring up Christopher Street and trying to gaze past the drove of pencil thin, denimed men congregating the streets.

"Dear Lord," Sheraton gulped, looking at Jeremy as he felt his mouth go dry. "Isn't that Mitch?"

"Not Mitch the Bitch?" Now it was Jeremy who felt his mouth grow dry.

Wearing double knit slacks that managed to be tight on the calves and several sizes too large around the waist and a shirt that was a symphony of polyester and rayon, was another friend of theirs.

"I thought I recognized you," Mitch called out, panting for breath as if he had been running to meet them. As eagerness to get together wasn't one of the strongest feelings in their friendship, Jeremy doubted it. "How come you're on the sidewalk and not in the gutter?"

Sheraton said. "It's been a long time."

"Not long enough," Jeremy added. "You shouldn't have gotten all dressed up for us. It must be a bitch caring for Sans-Belt slacks now that they're collectors items." Jeremy wondered why Mitch hadn't bothered to wash his face which looked pasty and scaly.

"So?" Mitch's pockets bulged with wallet and assorted papers. "I got all dolled up. Don't go get your jockstrap in an uproar. You're not dressed any better than I am."

"At least my shirt and pants don't look like they've taken on a personality of their own."

"What's wrong with my threads? If I had bought them from some queer, fairy bastard in Bloomingdale's you'd be happy?"

"Mitch," Jeremy said. "Cheap polyester becomes you and don't let anyone tell you differently."

Jumping in, Sheraton fairly yelled out: "What a surprise to see you down here."

"I don't usually come this far downtown," Mitch huffed, wiping his brow with a dirty handkerchief. "The Village doesn't agree with me."

"The Village doesn't agree with you and you don't sit too well with the rest of humanity so it's a fair swap," Jeremy said.

Surprisingly, Mitch ignored the barbed comment and asked: "Either of you two see Jazz around here?"

"Jazz asked you to meet him down here?" Sheraton was now the one to feel amazed. In his time, Jazz had done some innocent but silly things but asking a homophobic like Mitch to come into the West Village was a new one even for scatter brained Jazz.

"Yeah. The stupid bastard-or if he's wearing a dress tonight, would that make him a bitch-wanted to get together for a few laughs—"

"Henceforth, your clothes," Jeremy said.

"Do they still shove hot shivs's up guy's asses around here when there's nothing else to do?" Mitch asked.

"Only on Bastille Day and national bank holiday's."

Sheraton felt that he was the referee. "So, what time are you suppose to meet Jazz and begin having fun?"

"Fun?" Mitch looked grossly at two men walking down the street together holding hands. "If you guy's think *this* is fun, you'd probably find the Ox-bow incident a laugh riot."

Mitch was too engrossed in watching the male carnage of bodies walking by, that he hardly remembered to answer Sheraton's question.

"Did you see the pants on that last fruit that passed us by? I could probably tell that he had to take a leak before he even knew it."

"Maybe he'd be appreciative if you were to tell him so," Jeremy suggested.

"I hear you guy's are doing real well in your marriage," Mitch said, trying to hurt Jeremy. "What are you up to now, your Crisco anniversary?"

"If we continue to make a go of it," Jeremy said, "we're going to start a family. If we have a kid, we'll name it after you."

"Thanks."

"If we have anal warts, we'll also name them after you."

Mitch kept looking all around him in an open, obvious way.

"Where the hell is that freak of nature?" He asked, checking his wristwatch. "I'm here."

"And they say prayers aren't answered," Jeremy sighed.

"Is there a place around here where we could get a drink or something?"

"There are many places around here where you could get a drink and something," Jeremy told him. He didn't relish the idea of taking Mitch into one of the gay watering holes any more than he liked the idea of going into one himself.

"Not for me," Mitch snapped. "I want a place where I can sit down, not have my pants pulled down."

Sheraton raced his mind into high gear to think of a bar that was both dark enough, and not specialized to any particular taste, where Mitch could do the least amount of verbal damage. Since their college days, Mitch was never happy unless he was saying something insulting-usually on the top of his lungs.

"Those guys are wearing cowboy shirts," Mitch said as the door to one of the bars pulled open and several men ambled out. "Maybe I should run to a pay phone and call Annie Oakley and see if she wants to join us."

Before they could stop him, Mitch had swung open the door and disappeared into the bar. Sheraton shrugged and followed after a moment's pause.

"No pussy in here," Mitch said as soon as they found him, leaning against the bar.

"Must be a lot like your wet dreams then," Jeremy said, signaling the bar tender for some service.

"Hey," Mitch complained, not bothering to lower his voice. Fortunately, the juke box covered up most of his words. "Don't try telling me I don't dig women because I do."

"It was a joke, Mitch," Sheraton rushed. "You've got to forgive Jeremy. You know how he gets when he hasn't seen a June Allyson movie for a few days."

"Yeah? Well, just tell your boy friend here to cut the gay crap. I don't like that kind of talk about me."

"*You* don't like gay talk, Mitch?" Jeremy was more amazed than angry. "You? The one who uses the word 'pansy' more often than you'll ever hear in a florist shop."

"Forget it," Mitch said as he wrapped his lips around the neck of the beer bottle in front of him. "Doesn't the juke box here play anything decent? I suppose I should be glad they're not playing old Judy Garland records."

"Next we'll be talking about Fire Island and lisps," Jeremy whispered in disgust.

"Aren't you drinking?" Mitch asked Jeremy. "All that whispering going on between you two. What's the matter? Can't lift up the bottle with that limp wrist of yours?"

"Be grateful this limp wrist isn't working it's way down that nasty throat of yours, Mitch."

"Call Lady Jazz," Mitch fairly ordered Sheraton. "I'm getting sick of waiting in this hell hole for him to show up."

Sheraton nodded, turned to go to the pay phones lined up against one wall under some posters that had faded from age, and stopped.

"He's outside," Sheraton said, turning back. "He looks—"

"Yeah?" Mitch seemed to be listening to Sheraton with only half a mind-fifty per cent more than Jeremy would have given him credit for having.

"Jeremy, something's wrong," Sheraton said.

Jeremy still hadn't swallowed his mouthful of beer when Sheraton started to push him out the door.

On the street, a fleeting image of a very tall, willowy woman in a tight silver skirt was seen by them running down the street.

"Jazz," Sheraton called out. The figure didn't hear him the first time so he called again.

This time, the person did here and stopped, turned and ran back to them.

"Oh my God!" Jazz's face was a wrecked smear of mascara and pancake make-up. "It's awful. Sheraton, it's horrible."

"Calm down," Sheraton said, gripping Jazz by both arms. Under the shimmery top of his dress, Sheraton could feel how cold Jazz was. "What happened?"

"It's...It's Gene," Jazz cried, naming yet another college buddy of theirs. "Oh God. It's Gene."

"Tell us," Jeremy ordered him, trying to shake the story out. "What happened to Gene?"

"He's dead," Jazz wailed. "He's been murdered. Brutally, horribly murdered."

Those were the last words they were able to get out of Jazz before, in a heap of perfume and silver lame, he fainted dead away on the street.

Two

Playing the hero was probably never an easy task. Jeremy and Sheraton weren't exactly ill-suited for the assignment, they just found it cumbersome (to say the least) to half-drag and half-carry Jazz back to their apartment.

Mitch, never known for being either thoughtful or helpful whenever, proved to be less so now. He walked behind them doing nothing more than shaking his head and staring at every passer-by and loudly denying knowing any of them.

"Mitch," Jeremy puffed as they finally managed to drag Jazz into the front vestibule of their apartment building. "You've been just no end of help here but, really, you should go home and take it easy now."

"What's this? You guy's giving an old friend the bum's rush? I want to hear what happened that made Jazz pass out like that."

"Come on up, Mitch." Sheraton was trying to juggle Jazz's left side and one of the high heeled slippers that had come off his foot at the same time. "We'll make some tea-"

"Tea? Who the hell are you expecting? The Queen Mother?"

"We have enough queen's here as it is without inviting any more," Jeremy said as they tried to revive Jazz. The man seemed to be falling in and out of a deeply shocked state. He muttered and whined but nothing he said was clear or understandable.

Going up to their apartment wasn't easy. The steps seemed steeper and Mitch still refused to do anything but follow them.

On the landing before their own, a door tentatively opened. Instead of the customary New York procedure-an eye poking out from a barely cracked open door-a young, Nordic looking woman emerged.

"What is going on here?" She felt that there should have been something better to say. The woman, Pris, had a nodding acquaintance with the two men for a year or so. In that time, she had delegated them both in her mind as quiet and somewhat self-contained in their passions as they hardly ever partied or had guests over. She had a fleeting acquaintance with Jeremy's music and, at quieter times, could hear Sheraton's printer reeling off pages and type script. That was it. It hadn't prepared Pris for see-ing her neighbors in a disheveled state, carrying a rather strange looking woman up the stairs.

Jazz's wig was half off and the skirt of the dress had caught on nails and been dragged through the streets grime enough so that it would never be wearable again.

For lack of anything better to do than to satisfy her curiosity, Pris helped the men up the last flight of stairs and even picked up Jeremy's house keys-after he had dropped them-and opened the door for them.

Inside, Jeremy arranged Jazz on the sofa while Sheraton chal-lenged himself to find a better way to revive Jazz than by calling his mother long distance to find out what to do.

Somewhere in the back of both their minds were the chilling words that Jazz had used to describe the death of a friend. It seemed that, in fainting, Jazz had managed to enable them to prolong the torment of actually accepting the statement.

"Where's Mitch?" Jeremy asked as Pris tried to pour some cold water down Jazz's throat.

"The odd looking man?" Pris seemed to have taken an instance dislike toward Mitch. Considering that the last woman he had dated joined a nunnery after their first meeting-one date with Mitch and she swore off sex forever-it wasn't that surprising.

"I think he went into your bedroom," Pris said as she loosened the imitation pearls that were tightly clutched about Jazz's throat.

"He's where?"

"Leave him alone, Jeremy," Sheraton ordered him. "It will keep him quiet for a few minutes."

"The way he's inspecting your apartment, you'd think he was never up here before," Pris said.

"He never was," Jeremy told her. "I'm not exactly enjoying the thought of having Mitch anywhere near where I have to eat or sleep."

"What are you complaining about," Pris asked him. "Did you see the way he looked at me? I've had guys try to look up my skirt before but never has a guy tried to look up my pants."

A crash sounded from the direction of their bedroom.

"Mitch," Jeremy angrily called. "What the hell are you doing in there?"

"Sorry," Mitch said, popping out and easily falling into a chair. "I sort of broke that ugly lamp on the bedside table when I went to hang up the phone."

"Who were you phoning?" Sheraton asked.

"Hey! Didn't you hear what Jazz said? Something about Gene being dead. I called up the Sanders."

"You called up Karen and Marty?" Jeremy groaned out the names of the couple. Much like Mitch, Gene and Jazz, Marty and Karen had gone to school with them. It was an unmatched sort of set that couldn't be easily defined or explained. At the time, it worked and that was as far as they explored the diversification of personalities.

"They'll be right over," Mitch said. "I hope you got something better to serve them than tea." Then, espying Pris, he put a quick, clumsy move on the woman.

"They've got three kids," Mitch said, fairly drooling in an obnoxious way.

"Don't let it give you any ideas," Pris said, hoping to stop his obvious, over-played come-on act toward her.

"The way Karen was screaming in the background about the cost of hiring a baby-sitter, you'd think they had parented the Mormon Tabernacle Choir instead of just three brats."

Pris was saved from having to defend Marty and Karen's children and the cost of their sitter by Jazz who fluttered impossibly long eye lashes and stirred on the sofa.

"Take it easy, baby." Sheraton administered comfort to his friend as best he could.

"What happened?" Mitch shouted, shoving Sheraton aside and pushing his own face directly in front of Jazz's. "You were suppose to meet me hours ago and you never showed up. Left me standing on a street corner-*and in this neighborhood too.* Then you come screaming as if you had just lost your panties about Gene being killed."

"It was horrible," Jazz said, weakly trying to sit up. He was so dazed and out of it, he didn't bother to question how he had gotten up to Sheraton and Jeremy's apartment. Instead, he just tried to balance himself unsteadily on one arm that was loaded down with bangle bracelets. "He-Gene-was murdered tonight. In his apartment. I...I found him there."

"You found him?" Sheraton felt that, though he was doing all to help Jazz that he could, it wasn't enough. Finding the body of a dead man-and a friend as well-was too much for someone as sensitive as Jazz to take.

"There was blood," Jazz said in a soft, inconstant voice that threatened to slip into hysterics. "Everywhere. Oh. Who could have done such a thing to him?"

Shrugging his shoulder, Mitch said: "Probably some faggot. You know how they were always out trying to get Gene into bed with them."

"Did you call the police?" Sheraton's mind was finally falling into some logical sense of order. "Jazz, did you notify the police about what happened?"

"No," Jazz said, reaching for the glass of water but only managing to spill it down the front of his dress. "I couldn't. Don't you see? I couldn't. I was too scared."

"Then they don't know that Gene is dead?" Jeremy asked.

"I don't know," Jazz said. "I screamed long and loud enough so that the world must have come running."

"Then we have to do something," Sheraton advised Jazz. "We have to call the police or, if anybody saw you, it will look bad for you."

"Maybe they won't recognize me if anybody did see me running away," Jazz sighed.

"A six foot tall man dressed in sequins and pearls?" Mitch laughed uproariously. "Believe me, they saw that."

"Why did you go there in the first place?" Jeremy asked Jazz.

"I don't remember." Jazz put one hand to his forehead and slipped the wig back into place. Jeremy could see that Jazz's nails and lips were painted a matching color. "I don't remember anything. I feel so strange."

"Of course you do," Sheraton said softly. "Lie down for a minute and try to relax."

"You're not going to call the police, are you?" Jazz had eyes that were layered with several colors so that they looked like a peacock's tail. Even through the smudged paint, Sheraton could see the fear in them.

"They're not going to do anything," Mitch barked. "And, don't worry about it, Jazz. I got it all arranged."

"You?" Pris looked doubtful. She sounded it too.

"I called up a pal of mine," Mitch said, with no apology for the excess amount of phone calls that he had made from his friends phone. "She'll be right over."

"She?" A strange, crawling coldness filtered over Jeremy.

"Yeah," Mitch said. "You remember Barbara, don't you?"

"Barbara?"

"She'll be right over and she'll straighten things out," Mitch said. "Things will be a lot different once Barbara gets her ass here."

"Much different," Jeremy groaned.

*   *   *

Marty and Karen seemed to get downtown in an awfully short amount of time. Or, Jeremy pondered as he helped Sheraton dig cups and saucers out of the cupboard, did he just lose track of everything?

"So," Karen said in her piercing voice that carried shrilly everywhere. "What happened to Gene?"

Mitch, sitting there as if this were the best entertainment value to be had, seemed to be laughing at everything when he wasn't trying to catch Pris' eye in a lewd, suggestive way.

"Jazz got himself all gussied up tonight and went over there."

"God," Karen cried out, assuming the worst. "That's awful!" As she spoke, her eyes traveled around the boy's apartment and carefully appraised everything. She stopped short of measuring the screen on the television, satisfying herself that Marty had purchased one just slightly larger, and seemed smug and secure now that she knew that Jeremy and Sheraton had acquired nothing that she coveted.

"The police know," Marty said, nervously running his hands through his wiry thick hair. He was a tall man who seemed perpetually destined to slumping himself down into a compact sized, harassed man of unlimited patience and heartaches. "They were there when we passed by in our car."

"Our *new* car," Karen corrected him, pausing from the act of shoveling teaspoon's of sugar into her coffee long enough to emphasis the word as much as it was possible to do so.

"The police were there and the place looked like a mad house." Marty was, Jeremy reasoned, probably the only other person besides Sheraton who could tell cold, blunt facts in such a way that most of the sting was taken out of them.

Jazz, sitting meekly in a corner of the sofa, seemed to have trouble swallowing his tea. By this time, he had taken off the elaborate wig. His own hair was androgynous enough so that it could pass readily for a short woman's shag cut. His features were soft and aquiline enough to also pass for a woman's without having to put on the amount of make-up that he usually did. Even his clothes were generally uni-sexually cut but with a decided pronouncement toward femininity.

"It was terrible," he said softly enough that he might have gone unheard.

"Try not to think about it," Sheraton instructed him. Then, turning to the rest of them, he asked: "Jeremy and I sort of lost touch with Gene lately. Was anything happening in his life?"

"You mean, was he doing anything that might have led him to be murdered?" Marty seemed to have trouble with this.

"We saw him a few weeks ago at a big party we gave," Karen started to say when she remembered something and stopped herself.

"It wasn't *that* large of a party," she continued, in way of apology to Sheraton and Jeremy who definitely had not been invited to the shindig.

"Gene was at your home recently," Sheraton said, wondering what God had favored he and Jeremy so that they hadn't made Karen's A list. "What's he been up to?"

"You know Gene," Karen said, ignoring her husband who seemed suddenly concerned with the conversation. "He was his usual silly self." She paused to grab a handful of cookies. "Sorry if I'm speaking ill of the dead and all that but, you all knew him. He was a strange man."

Jeremy thought back. It wasn't that long ago but it was difficult all the same. The recollections were all there but none of them wanted to come easily to mind.

"You're what?"

Gene had a way of half-screaming, half-shouting everything-especially if it didn't suit him.

He had been their friend. In college, it was through Gene that he and Sheraton had first met and became acquainted.

While they had to go through the difficult, trying process of coming to terms with their budding sexual preference, they had an even larger problem in dealing with Gene and his hostilities.

No one had ever seen Gene with a woman-or a man for that matter. Yet, he was decidedly heterosexual-especially in the vocal sense.

They knew that he wouldn't accept the news of their discovering each other easily. Still, Sheraton reasoned that they had already wasted their teen's playing games with themselves. Why, he persuaded a reluctant Jeremy, play the same games for the rest of our lives? We love each other and there is no disgrace in good, honest love.

Standing in Washington Square Park with Gene on a Sunday afternoon was not the ideal time to come out of the closet. Still, that's the way it happened.

Jeremy, the usually quiet one, took in a deep breath and let out the story in an impossibly short sentence.

Gene stared at them, shouted and then walked away. For the reason that he didn't want to break too many ties with his past, Jeremy followed Gene to the subway station.

"Listen," Jeremy said breathlessly. "You've got to understand. This doesn't change our friendship at all. It's a mind boggler, I'll grant you. Still, you can't blame us for being dishonest. We're leveling with you."

"Fucking faggot shits," Gene said, enjoying the amplification that the West Fourth Street subway tunnel gave to his voice. "Fucking faggots. No wonder I don't have that many friends. They probably all knew you and Sheraton were queer and that's why they didn't have anything to do with me."

"You had us, Gene," Jeremy said, only today realizing that he had used the past tense when speaking. "We were your friends."

"Faggots can't be friends with other guys. They only think of one thing."

After that, college ended. He and Sheraton, luckily, didn't. They didn't see the friends they saw every day during school all that frequently. It was an easier transition than they would have thought. People like Marty and Karen-college sweethearts-contacted them sporadically. Gene was a man they only met at other people's parties or weddings. He always greeted them, and then quickly mocked them-both behind their backs and to their faces.

Somehow, Sheraton managed to make it seem like a very small loss. But that was when Gene was alive; with them; with a hope that one day they could move forward and try to forget what had happened and what Gene had said.

"Still didn't have a good thing to say about anybody but himself," Karen was saying when Jeremy shook himself out of his deep thoughts. "Always right no matter how wrong he was. And, such a liar—"

"Karen," Marty meekly intoned, trying to stop his wife.

"Oh, but it's true," Karen shrilled. "I mean, I'm sorry he's dead and all but, he wasn't a lovable guy."

Jeremy remembered so many things now.

Impossibly tall and startlingly thin, Gene was far from handsome. He also had a stand-offish quality that alienated himself from others. His selfish snobbery didn't win him any friends or a life but it gave him a mystic quality that made people wonder about him. Soon, in some cases,

*the wonder turned to curiosity and Gene insisted, turned into infatuation
toward him.*

"How come you were there?" Mitch looked at Jazz. Jazz wasn't in
a mood to be nagged for an answer and that was a question-
although pertinent-that bothered him.

"He was all right," Jazz said. Sheraton knew that Jazz was lying.
There was something more, something that had been strongly
omitted from his words. But what?

The doorbell rang. Pris, eager to escape from Mitch's hands that
seemed constantly shoving themselves dangerously near her blouse,
jumped up to answer it.

"That must be Barbara," Mitch said, helping himself to another
cookie.

"Barbara?" Karen said the word as others might swear.

"Hey, baby, Barbara's good people. You just got to give her a
chance."

"A chance?" Karen looked at Jeremy. "The only thing I'd like to
give that bitch is a one-way ticket to Hell."

"Don't waste your money," Jeremy told her. "She'll get there in
her own sweet time."

*   *   *

Pris, an accurate minded person who was able to deduce a person's makeup logically and-for the most part-accurately, was
beginning to find Jeremy and Sheraton to be smooth men who
were simple enough so that some urbane sophistication hadn't
polished off their common, likable traits.

She could find little in the likes of either Karen or Mitch to
redeem them in her eyes.

It was the sudden appearance of Barbara, striking a ridiculous pose in the doorway, that led her to believe that none of this was happening-it was all a dream and a silly one at that.

"Mitch," Barbara husked as she stood there in a too-tight black dress with a straw, wide-brimmed hat covering a good portion of her face. "How terribly awful."

Through a mouthful of cookie, Mitch responded with: "Yeah baby. Crime generally is."

"The only crime that's been committed is the price that acne faced teen-age girls charge to sit for you on the spur of the moment," Karen cried. "And, if you want to know who should be murdered it's those damn cleaning ladies. They charge so much you think they have master's degree's in dusting-not that they could dust to save their lives. God forbid you should ask them to do a little something more like make dinner for twelve or hem up a couple of your dresses-they actually think they should be paid extra for that!"

"So much for domestic bliss and harmony," Barbara said tartly. "A pox on all their houses."

"Barbara," Jeremy said in his short-hand way of cutting immediately to the quick of things. "What are you doing here?"

"Come off it, Jeremy," Mitch shouted. "You know how Barbara felt about Gene."

"She felt he was really the Son of Sam and that the other guy was just covering up for him."

"That was then," Barbara said, falling into a chair and hiking up her skirt to show short, rather plain legs. "This is now. Things have changed between us; surely you must have heard?"

"Do you have any Ring-Ding's?" Mitch asked.

"I'd like to ring-ding your neck," Jeremy hissed.

"Jeremy's right," Karen piped in. "Why would you invite Sister Scum here at a time like this? Also, how did she get here? Does her latest psycho ward have revolving doors?"

"She's OK now," Mitch said quickly. "And she and Gene had gotten pretty tight."

Sheraton listened but didn't bother to debate the point. There were many pro's and con's that could be said about Barbara-the con's outweighing the pro's by a considerable margin. Like the others, she was also a college acquaintance but one they kept clear of generally.

She was an intelligent, sometimes witty, woman who had burnt out too quickly. She lived her life fast and hard and couldn't keep up with her set pace.

When they met her, Barbara was prone to fighting, vulgarity and trips into fantasy that she confused with reality.

"I came," Barbara said slowly, "because, despite it all, we are friends. At a time like this, I do need my friends around me for support. What would I do without you wonderful people? Oh, and you too Karen."

"What you need is a gag," Karen barked.

"What are you carrying on about?" Marty asked Barbara.

"I'm hardly carrying on about anything," Barbara answered. "I'm here to be with all my friends and loved one's in this, the darkest hour of my life."

Karen gave a loud snort.

"Second darkest hour of my life," Barbara corrected herself. "The first was when I met Karen and that will go unequaled."

"Everybody's very upset and shaken up about what happened," Pris said, looking especially at Jazz now. He seemed the weak one- the man who couldn't defend himself any more than he could accept what had happened.

"But, I need my friends," Barbara wailed. "I tell you, I cannot go on. I can't live."

"Don't fight the urge," Karen said.

"Karen, I just lost the only man that I ever, truly loved. Have you no heart? Have you no compassion? Have you no desire to diet and lose that fat ass?

"One day, perhaps God will smile down upon you and give you a man to love. Until then, just try to be understanding, kind and compassionate to all human beings. And, wear a long line bra while you're at it."

Karen had blood in her eyes. "Look Barbara, I don't know what your shrink has you on this week but I am not buying any of this three act play you're trying to perform.

"You couldn't stand Gene's guts when he was alive. He hated you like the turd that you are. So, what is all this, 'Oh my man I love him so' nonsense?"

"Karen, I happen to have been Gene's lover." Barbara pulled out an elaborately jeweled art-deco compact and began to put her make up on as she spoke. "Some people do have a sex life you know.

"So, if you persist in insulting both myself and the memory of my late lover, I must ask you to step outside-preferably in front of a speeding bus."

"That's not true," Karen complained. "Gene hated you."

"My," Barbara said, studying her face in the compact's mirror. "You seem to speak as if you were awfully close to Gene. Just how well did you know him?"

Karen whitened and pressed her lips together.

"You," Barbara pronounced, "are not fit to live with pigs."

"Take that back."

"Forgive me," Barbara apologized. "You *are* fit to live with pigs."

"Look Barbara," Jeremy said heatedly. "This is not the time or the place to start a petty argument."

"I've been accused of being many things but never petty."

"Now you have a new one to add to the ever growing list," Jeremy continued. "Right now, a friend has died. No one is leaving here under your say so. But, if you want to see somebody going out the door—"

Jeremy finished with an elaborate gesture.

"You too?" Barbara said softly to Jeremy. "Don't any of you have any idea of the shocking blow I've had tonight?

"The only man that I shall ever love was taken away from me. Can't you show me some respect or, are you all too jealous of me? Did you all want Gene for yourselves? Is that it? Do you begrudge me for the happiness I allowed him to have?"

"You and Gene being lovers is certainly a new one," Sheraton said. "I'll admit that we didn't keep in close contact with him—"

"None of his supposed friends kept in touch with him," Barbara snapped. "Perhaps if you had, maybe if you had taken the time and had the decency to be patient with him, you might have gotten to know the man like I did.

"No. You were all too concerned with coming out of closets and hiring baby sitters. None of you cared for Gene or cared about him. You were all too concerned about yourselves to even stop to think about him.

"That's where it was different and why I was so important to Gene. I loved him. Honest, mature love. Isn't that right, Mitch?"

"They fucked like bunnies," Mitch said.

"Sheer poetry," Karen snarled. "And we thought it was only an affair like you, Barbara. Cheap."

"Gene is dead," Jazz said. "It doesn't matter who loved him. He's gone, murdered."

"Yes," Barbara said firmly. "He's dead. And I shall hunt down his killer if it's the last thing I do.

"None of you understands what it is like for a woman to be loved by a man. Especially you, Karen."

"Shut your mouth," Karen warned her.

"You and Gene were having an affair?" Marty asked. "How come he never told any of us about it?"

"Tell any of you?" Barbara put one hand to her chest and feigned surprise. "He couldn't tell you because he had to put on a show."

"Gene put on a show," Jeremy said. "That's something you're pretty good at, Barbara."

"When was the last time any of you gave me a chance?" Barbara shouted. "I was only the woman who had a couple of nervous break-downs and some shock treatments. You never gave me a chance. You all hate me and won't allow me to prove myself.

"Gene knew how you all felt. You think he was harsh but, he wasn't. He wanted your love and your friendship. He thought he needed it. He tried to keep both you-and himself-happy by putting our affair in the shadows."

"He should have put it in *The Twilight Zone*," Karen said.

"Karen, I hope one day you will have as many brains as you do chins," Barbara said. "It's the animosity and hatred that you shower me with that was the reason why Gene and I couldn't be open about our love for each other. To show my love and prove it to Gene, I agreed not to make public my true feelings toward him."

"That's all well and good," Pris said to Barbara. "But, right now, I wouldn't go solving any mysteries on your own. That's a case for the police."

"The police," Barbara echoed. "Yes. I've already spoken to them."

"You did what?" Karen screamed.

"I was no end of help to them," Barbara went on. "I gave them all your names and phone numbers-both at home and the office. Although I'm sure they'll bring Gene's killer to a trial, I also shall help solve this case."

"Just what every murder case needs," Jeremy hissed. "Robo Psycho."

Standing up and grabbing Mitch's arm as she did so, Barbara announced: "The police shall be in touch with all of you." She looked at Karen, Marty and Jazz especially. "Friday night is the wake. I expect you all to be there."

"Why?" asked Jeremy, one who hadn't planned on attending.

"Only the guilty parties will stay away," Barbara said. "The police already informed me of that. I can't wait to see which of you will be too racked with guilt not to show your face there."

"That woman is crazy," Marty said after Barbara and Mitch had departed.

"Crazy," Pris said, collecting their coffee cups. "But also accurate. I bet the police will be at the funeral Friday and take attendance."

Jeremy groaned.

THREE

A hazy, gauze-like film settled over Jeremy and Sheraton. It was a dream; it couldn't be anything else but a dream.

Pris, finding her neighbors friendly and suddenly realizing the impossibly wide gulf that one floor created between them, tried to talk to them. It was the beginning of a funny, warm but quirky relationship.

Jeremy found Pris' caustic wit and sharp tongue to be a match to his although he felt neither threatened or bothered by it. Sheraton, friendly and always amiable to strangers, was in his element. He showed Pris the gifts his mother constantly showered he and Jeremy with, prompting Pris to say, "She sent you a VCR? Do you think you could put in a good word for me? I need a microwave oven." He also discussed his boyhood up-bringing (and manhood ties) to Wisconsin.

Friday dawned and with it both men felt that a new chapter was being written into their lives.

"We're too young to be going to funerals for our peers," Jeremy explained, stumbling his fingers over a jar of currant jam. "This is something our parents have in their lives, not us."

But, it did occur in their lives. They had a funeral to attend and, soberly and without much certainty in either justice or fate, they attended.

It was a nightmare for Sheraton. He suddenly found himself tongue tied and awkward. Jeremy managed to walk through it, barely, by pretending that he was an author plotting a funeral scene for a book.

"This is a heavy scene," Marty said, falling down beside them and mopping his brow despite the amplified air-conditioning system. "Karen wants to know if you're free to go out for coffee after this."

Sheraton agreed before Jeremy could protest. In his wise eyes, Sheraton figured something out. Marty was upset by something and Gene's funeral was only a small part of it.

Sitting on Tenth Avenue, shrouded in darkness but filled with yuppie couples loudly talking, they found an outside table at The Empire Diner.

Stainless steel was behind them; the pre-requisite of an empty Perrier bottle with a dried flower leaning over the lip was on the small table in front of them.

"Do you believe that Barbara?" Karen said as she fanned herself with the laminated menu. "A black dress and a hat with a veil! The last woman who got away with wearing a veil was Eleanor Roosevelt."

"That bothers me," Marty said. He was bothered by many things tonight. The price that the Empire Diner charged for a cup of coffee was one of them. "What is Barbara doing carrying on about Gene? And, why is she talking to the police?"

"Did the police contact you?" Karen said, sitting stiffly in her chair. She tried to ignore most of the street traffic but found herself oddly displaced. She was use to gossipy, casual lunches with the girls. In her mind, she had a definite rule of where to eat and where not to. Tenth Avenue and Twenty Second Street wasn't one of the prime locations in her book.

"They contacted us all right," Marty said. "You wouldn't believe the questions they asked us."

"Why bother you?" Jeremy wasn't being merely loyal. He couldn't picture anybody accusing Marty of anything more serious than never being able to wear the right tie with his shirt.

"I'll tell you why," Karen hissed. "It's that bitch Barbara. She's suddenly playing Nancy Drew. If the police had any sense, she's the one they'd be investigating."

"Barbara is a killer without a gun," Sheraton said. "She's unbalanced but hardly a killer. You know that."

"I don't put anything past that broad," Karen huffed. She was one who never liked to defend her ideas, even when they were presented with reasons to back them up.

It came as a surprised, although it should have been guessed, when Barbara and Mitch walked up to them.

"Thank you for coming to the funeral," Barbara said, her voice fluky and thick as if the veil covering her face was disguising it. "I want each of you to know just how much it means to me that you showed up to give me your moral support."

"Wake up and read the reviews," Karen said. Her mood was darkened considerably when she realized that Mitch had dragged two additional chairs to the table and that he and Barbara were planning on joining them. "Nobody was clapping after your performance, Barbara. Your tears and sobs as you had to be escorted away from the casket were all for naught. In the future, try to remember that old Rialto saying, 'Farce closes on a Saturday night'."

Barbara lifted her veil and let it rustle in the wind. "How quaint and fortunate for all of us. Karen is now going to entertain us with her remembrances about the nights she spent walking around Times Square."

"The only one I feel sorry for is Jazz," Sheraton said. "Did you see how upset he was?"

"It's just the shock of never seeing him without his Blush-And-Glo on," Marty said, grinding a small packet of sugar substitute between his fingers.

"Why did you even bother to go to the funeral?" Karen asked Barbara.

"Why, to observe all you," she answered simply. "I suppose that those of you with brains have figured out the circumstances surrounding the death of my beloved."

"Don't get into it now," Mitch suggested.

"I'm sure the police will be able to take care of this," Marty said.

"They're not even interested," Barbara complained, her voice rising causing several other patrons to look at her. "No visible sign of forced entry. No reports from the neighbors of an argument. No signs of a struggle.

"Oh. It will be so easy for the cops to forget the whole thing."

"That's not true," Jeremy said, firmly believing it.

"They think that one of us killed him," Marty said, barely avoiding the caustic look his wife was giving him. "They feel that Gene knew who his attacker was and let him in of his own free will."

"Thinking he was a friend," Barbara added.

"Or a lover?" Karen smiled.

"Give the poor kid a break," Mitch ordered Karen. "She just lost her lover."

"And we lost a friend," Marty said angrily. "Barbara isn't the only one who suffered a loss. Did any of you happen to notice Gene's family at the funeral?"

"Oh, them," Barbara said fitfully.

"Yes," Karen said. "The one's who were shedding real tears."

"Gene wasn't given a ticket for jay walking," Barbara said. "He was murdered. This is serious, Karen. Why are you trying to make a joke out of it? Are you afraid of something?"

"If you ever get a job, apply for a position as executive in charge of production," Karen suggested strongly. "You make a big production out of everything you do."

"How about we order?" Marty said, trying to end at least the latest confrontation. "Coffee and Danish?"

"Coffee and Danish!" Barbara cried out. "Anything for the adults?"

"Only for the adults who are planning on paying for themselves," Karen stated.

"Marty," Barbara gasped. "Am I to gather from all your wife's mooing that you won't even give a poor, grieving widow a cup of coffee unless she pays for it herself?"

"You got it," Karen roared.

"Even after I've cried," Barbara said. "Why, just feel my cheeks."

"Feel your cheeks? Sure honey. Right after you kiss my-"

"Karen," Sheraton said. "It's OK. Jeremy and I will pick up the tab for coffee and cake."

"Lucky us," Jeremy muttered.

"You needn't bother," Barbara said to Sheraton. "Mitch will pay for us."

Mitch gulped the air and looked pea green at the suggestion.

"We'll pay," Marty nimbly suggested.

"Thank you," Barbara said, reaching out and petting Marty's hand. "I guess opposites do attract."

"One more word out of you and my fist is going to attract with your jaw," Karen said.

"Have we been sitting her for an awful long time?" Marty asked. "There's somebody looking like they want our table."

Sheraton didn't know why but he turned about and saw a face that rang a vague, distant bell in his mind.

"Isn't that Alan, Gene's younger brother?" Jeremy said.

"So it is," Sheraton said, suddenly feeling an odd mixture of excitement and anticipation. "So it is."

Barbara popped up quickly.

"Come Mitch," she said to her companion. "We must be going."

Mitch, hardly about to leave when he had two offers to pay for his coffee looming, protested.

"I don't want to be here with Alan," she said flatly. "Gene hated his family." Turning to the others, she said: "They're a bunch of ingrates and phonies. If any of you had any brains, you'd refuse him if he asks to join you."

"I won't do that," Sheraton said. "I think that, tonight, he needs a friend."

"Friend!" Mitch said the word with a dirty insinuation.

"Yes Mitch. Friend."

Barbara's tugging finally had it's desired effect and Mitch stood up to depart.

Looking over his shoulder, he saw Alan asking to sit with them. Loudly he said:

"Ah. Ain't love grand?"

*   *   *

It seemed that as soon as Gene's brother Alan asked to join them, the other members of the party went fleeing off into the night.

Karen and Marty suddenly had a similar flash of the mental calculations of how much the baby sitter would be charging them and, rather brusquely, they departed leaving Jeremy and Sheraton to face off with Alan in a sort of odd-numbered tete-a-tete.

Condolences were passed across the table to Alan by Sheraton while Jeremy took the moment to study the young man.

He was tall and lanky in a sort of unfinished way. His neck was pencil thin and his Adam's apple bobbed wildly up and down whenever he spoke. His eyes were pale blue to the point of near transparency and his hair was a weak shade of brown and looked as if it had been cut by Alan himself with a pair of dull scissors.

"It's a shock," Alan was saying when Jeremy tuned into the conversation. "Of course, if you knew my brother, you'd have known that something like this was going to happen."

"We met your brother," Sheraton carefully said to the boy. "We knew him but not all that well."

"Not surprising," Alan said, fidgeting nervously with the starched collar of his baggy, white shirt. "Most people generally didn't want to get to know Gene once they had a sampling of him."

"He was determined and rather hard headed," Jeremy heard Sheraton respond. He was glad that Sheraton was handling this. He couldn't think of a kinder way to put it. "I suppose that it put some people off."

"It put everybody off Gene," his brother said sadly. "Including his family.

"Look, I've got to tell this to somebody. Gene wasn't one of the nicest people around."

"He had a very good side to him," Sheraton honestly replied, speaking as one who wasn't necessarily defending the reputation of the dearly departed but truly had seen glimmering's of it in the past. "He could be warm, funny and quite friendly."

Alan looked as if he wanted to believe that but he still shook his head in denial.

"He *pretended* to be all those things. You have to understand something about Gene. He was jealous and got a vicarious thrill out of hurting other people."

"So," Jeremy said. "You think that your brother's jealous rages might have been the cause of his death?"

Alan stared blankly across the table at them. It had taken him a moment or two to collect himself from Jeremy's blunt introduction to a topic that he, more than likely, had intended to introduce eventually.

"Those other people who were sitting here before I came; who were they?"

"Friends of your brother," Sheraton told him.

"Was one of them Joshua?"

Sheraton had to stop and think for a moment. Joshua was most definitely a name he had encountered earlier but where? Then, it struck him.

"Jazz?" He had so seduced himself into the nickname that he had long ago stopped using the Christian name even when he sent Christmas cards. "No. Jazz didn't want to get together afterward."

"But he was at the funeral, wasn't he?"

"Yes," Sheraton answered, curious why Jazz alone should have peaked Alan's curiosity. Was it the drag aspect of it?

"He was there. Sitting in a corner. Shallow skinned and slightly anemic looking," Jeremy said, leaving out the fact that Jazz and Alan could almost pass for brothers a lot more easier than Alan and Gene could.

"I heard about him," Alan explained. "Gene denied having any friends. He only talked about Jazz."

"Then your brother never told you about his girl friend?" Jeremy wondered what effect that would have on Alan.

He blinked, seemed oddly displaced, and then blinked again.

"Gene didn't have a girl friend. Or, I didn't think he had one. You see, Gene didn't like to be touched. I can't see any guy getting involved in a relationship without touching."

Jeremy's mind was running down the same track as Sheraton's. Neither of them could remember even shaking hands with Gene. What Alan was saying might be so.

"The woman in the veil," Alan said. "The strange girl. Does she claim to be my brothers girl friend?"

"Keep in mind the word strange," Jeremy advised Alan. "It will make it all the easier when you have to consider Barbara and her claims."

"He may have had a girl friend," Alan said in a pensive tone. He wanted company now more than he wanted to talk. Still, he felt some polite, social obligation to them and so he continued.

"We didn't see Gene all that often. To be truthful about it, he always caused such a commotion when he came to visit the family, none of us pushed invitations upon him. Not that we stopped him from coming over."

"The last time you saw him," Sheraton said. "Did he say something that gave you the slightest impression that he was becoming involved with somebody?"

"A lot of things happened the last time he came over," Alan said. "I don't want to talk about them though."

"You had a fight with him?" Jeremy asked.

"We always had a fight whenever Gene was in the room," Alan said quickly. "No matter what the occasion, he was always there with his boxing gloves on-figuratively."

"The part about Gene's having a girl friend. What gave you that impression, Alan?"

"Things he said," Alan admitted. "I don't remember his exact words and I don't think it ever helps to paraphrase somebody. Gene and I got into a fight...I don't want to talk about *that*. We just had words. Before he went, I said something to Gene like, 'You're going to die a lonely man if you keep going on being so difficult and argumentative' and he laughed at me. Then he said something like, 'Oh, don't worry about me. I've got somebody. '

"That surprised me to no end. I mean, I was really happy that Gene might have finally found somebody but he didn't make it sound like a lover sort of set-up. Then he said, 'I'm going to make out all right with this one. I've been kicked around a lot by the whole bunch of you. Now I'm in control and I'm going to start being treated right.'"

"What do you think he meant by that?" Sheraton asked, having some wild ideas on the subject but wanting to hear Alan's theories.

"My brother was a complainer. According to mom, he always was one. Everything had to be done for him. He couldn't understand why the world didn't revolve around him. As he got older, many people tried to tell him that people would treat him better if he treated them nicer. He didn't buy that. He felt that they had to dance for him and all he had to do was sit back and accept their gifts.

"Not wanting to be touched and all seems to fit into things. He didn't want love-not physical love certainly and probably not the security of emotional love either. He wanted slaves who would idolize him and put him up on a pedestal but be afraid to touch him because he was so valuable."

Jeremy and Sheraton had earlier discussed how Gene had managed to create an aloofness around himself that made people curious to get closer to him. Now, with Alan's words in their ears, it didn't seem like a fluke accident. It seemed more like an intentional arrangement that Gene had worked out for himself.

"Why did you mention Jazz?" Sheraton asked. "Or Joshua."

Alan looked as if he wanted to shrug it off but he said, "Jazz was infatuated with my brother. That part didn't seem all that strange to me. What did strike me as odd was that Gene allowed Jazz to be anywhere near him. You must know how my brother felt about homosexuals?"

Jeremy let out a slight groan that got carried away with the wind but not before Alan could hear it.

"He hated gay's," Jeremy said. "He was rather vocal about it."

"Too vocal," Alan agreed. "That's why I was surprised that he continued the friendship with Jazz.

"You know Jazz. What has he said about all this?"

"He's upset," Sheraton said. His words were guarded. He suddenly felt that Alan was fishing for answers but he didn't quite know what the questions were or how the boy would use the answers if they were provided to him. "He's had a rough time in dealing with this. All of us have."

"I dropped by Gene's place one night," Alan said. "I met Jazz there. I only met him for a minute before Gene gave me the bum's rush and practically threw me out but I sort of liked the guy."

"He's sweet," Sheraton agreed, all the while wondering what would bring Alan to Gene's place when it was a fact that they didn't get along.

"So, Jazz hasn't said anything?"

Jeremy immediately picked up that this was a point that was bothering Alan. But why?

"He's not a strong person," Jeremy said. "He can't handle this sort of thing."

"Then it's best to just leave him alone," Alan smiled. "That would be best for all, wouldn't it?"

Sheraton smiled but made sure he didn't nod in agreement.

The last thing he had any intentions of doing was *not* to speak to Jazz about his relationship with both Gene and Alan.

*   *   *

Going home meant, to Jeremy, a night of rest. The toll of the week was weighing heavily upon him and, he felt, it must be having the same effect upon Sheraton.

Once home, Sheraton found himself filled with an impatient amount of nervous energy. He tried to relieve it, at first, through domestic channels.

He set up the tea kettle, bought the water to a boil and seeped the loose tea for five minutes under a cozy-all courtesy of his mother. Jeremy filled a plate with blueberry muffins-courtesy of Enterman's Bakery.

First Pris from downstairs came up to visit for a late night chat. There was the aura of a friendly, concerned woman that struck both men immediately. Beneath that, they were beginning to see the growing bud's of comradeship.

"I know that today must have been tough on you," she said while waiting impatiently for the tea to seep. "Especially with that Mitch character. How ever do you stand him?"

"He's not important," Jeremy told her, breaking open a muffin and chewing it before the tea. "He's a sick, loud mouth who's better left ignored. I think that was his parent's motto. Of course, Barbara was no better."

Sheraton's mind was turning and rolling over repeatedly with the various names. All of them seemed to mean something. People he knew but hardly thought about suddenly seemed foreigners to him.

"What's up?" Jeremy caught the look in Sheraton's eyes immediately.

"I've got something to show you," Sheraton said, walking over to the computer, turning it on and pulling up a database program to the screen.

"Marty, Karen, Barbara, Jazz and Mitch." Jeremy read the names without putting any obvious connection between them for a moment.

"Those are the people who knew that friend of yours," Pris said. "Gene, wasn't it?"

"You spent three thousand bucks to write down the names of people we went to school with," Jeremy said quizzically. He knew Sheraton better than this. There was something brewing other than the tea.

"You're the great mystery novel reader in the family," Sheraton said as he pushed some function keys. "Don't you see anything strange in Gene's death?"

"I suppose that Alan's words are marked on your mind," Jeremy sighed. "After reading every Agatha Christie and Ngaio Marsh I could get my hands on, I already thought of the odd thread before you did. The only thing is, that's in murder mysteries. It's not real. These plots and sub-plots don't happen in real life, Sheraton."

"Jazz and Gene were friends," Sheraton said, typing as he spoke. "Gene hated gay's. You could hardly accuse Jazz of being anything but gay. That doesn't strike you as an odd acquaintance?"

"I suppose next you'll be reciting to me all those lies that Barbara is trying to peddle. Sheraton, dead men really can't tell tales. She can say anything now. Gene can't call her a liar to her face." Jeremy turned and looked at Pris. "Besides, he called her a lot worse things while he was alive."

"She's certainly out to have us believe that they had an affair going," Sheraton coyly said. "Doesn't that make you suspicious?"

"The woman is nuts. Crazy. Why listen to her?"

"OK," Sheraton conceded. "How about Marty and Karen?"

"Now you're stretching the limits of even the most fertile of imaginations." Jeremy sighed and, without consulting the kitchen timer first, poured out three cups of tea. "You're certainly not going to accuse Karen of anything worse than being short waisted, are you?"

"They're acting awfully funny."

"So are you, lover boy."

"I'm concerned," Sheraton reasoned. "Are they?"

"They looked worried," Pris admitted. "However, there was something odd about their concern."

"What?" Sheraton prompted her.

"I don't know," Pris said, sitting down and balancing her tea cup precariously on her lap. "It was as if something were bothering the both of them. But, do you want to hear something really weird? I don't think that they were both worried about the same thing."

"Exactly," Sheraton said. "And, Pris, you didn't even hear what Gene's brother Alan had to say."

"He didn't really say anything," Jeremy corrected his lover.

"Why did he follow us then?" Sheraton pointed out. "He left his family and followed us. Why?"

"Because he was looking for Jazz." Jeremy said it before he actually thought about the implications of the statement that he had only thought about in an obvious, unassuming way. "Why would he want Jazz that badly?"

"And what was Jazz doing in Gene's apartment that night?" Pris' voice was almost giddy with excitement. "If Gene hated gays then why would Jazz bother spending time with Gene-especially when Jazz was dressed in drag."

The excitement of the moment was trying to lug Jeremy with the flow.

"This is crazy," he said, gaining some control over himself. "Do you have any idea of just what you are implying?"

"Somebody killed Gene," Pris said. "It stands to reason that, from what the police told your friends already, Gene had to know who his killer was. If Gene knew, then perhaps you know too."

Jeremy fought a mad desire to begin pacing around in a circle. "That's ridiculous. We went to college with these people. We cheated off one another. We cut classes together."

"So?" Pris asked. "You think that maybe the Boston Strangler had a perfect attendance record when he went to school?"

"Marty and Karen can't do anything more lethal than buying polyester and handing them out for Christmas gifts. Jazz's only crime is teasing his wigs so high that they create obstacle courses for low flying planes.

"These are normal people. They're our friends. Do you realize that you're saying that they're killers?"

"You'd trust either Mitch or Barbara with a lethal weapon?" Pris said.

"They're two pathetic fools," Jeremy insisted. "People that we know don't commit murder."

"People we know aren't killed either," Sheraton said softly. He stood up and put an arm around Jeremy. "Or so we thought."

"Sheraton, this has been a big blow to you."

"I was wondering when you would start talking dirty to one another in front of me," Pris smiled.

"I'm serious," Jeremy told her.

"I'm a dyke," she told him. "It still doesn't mean that we can't come into contact with killers."

"Our friends?" Jeremy stared at the names in perfect VGA color on the monitor in front of him. "You think one of our friends killed Gene?"

"Maybe," Sheraton said slowly. "Just maybe."

FOUR

No matter how vigorously he exercised, how many cups of coffee he drank or how hard he tried, Jeremy awoke that Saturday morning feeling as if cobweb's had filled his head and jammed up his functioning process.

Sheraton, restraining himself from bringing up the discussion that they had started the previous evening, suggested that they go for a long walk.

Walking wasn't a usual hobby for Jeremy but, with Sheraton chattering along side him, he found it a pleasant diversification from the ordinary. They walked throughout the Village-both east and west-through SoHo and Tribeca and had lunch at an arty-and vastly overpriced-popular spot of the moment on a street that had once seen only weekday factory life keeping it alive. Now, men in torn pants and unpressed shirts pulled out silver or gold American Express cards to pay for their repasts.

Walking home, Sheraton kept up a continuous line of conversation that centered innocently on the changing face of the city. Jeremy noticed, but didn't comment, on how Sheraton steered clear of any talk of Gene or his list of suspects.

Reaching their block, Sheraton stopped talking in mid-sentence and reached for Jeremy's arm.

"The police are parked half on the sidewalk in front of our building," he said, immediately forcing his feet to move.

"They've come to question us about Gene," Jeremy said, running along side of him. "Now remember, none of that nonsense you started in last night. I mean, you're beginning to sound like something out of that old Bob Seeger song about mysteries without any clues. You have a mystery but that's all you have and the mystery is not even yours."

But it wasn't a routine investigation that had brought the police officers there.

Pris, looking pale and startled, sat just within the vestibule with her hands clasped around her knees.

"What's the matter?" Sheraton felt such a close kinship to the woman that he was immediately on the verge of offering her a shoulder to cry upon.

"I went to knock on your door," she said in a confused tone. "The only trouble is, your door was half off it's hinges when I got there."

"Somebody broke into our place?" Jeremy was half up the steps before he had the entire sentence out of his mouth.

Upstairs, the police were walking around their apartment. Books, records and nearly every object that had ever been stuffed into a closet was scattered across the floor.

"Never seen anything quite like this," one of the officers finally admitted. He tipped his hat back and let out a low whistle. "They were really looking for something here. Think they found it?"

Put on his guard, Jeremy said: "We have nothing that anybody could possibly want."

After the police left, Pris stood on without asking and began to pick up things and looked for a spot to place them.

"What were they looking for?" she asked, not anymore satisfied with Jeremy's answer than the police probably were.

"I don't know," Jeremy sighed, his hands stuffed with papers and books. "Maybe Jimmy Hoffa. Whoever did this looked into cabinets that even I didn't know we had."

"Maybe I should run downstairs and get my Hoover," Pris suggested.

"Hoover? What we need is a dump trunk."

She tried to smile but found it too depressing to even fake the action.

"Pris," Sheraton said as he sorted and sifted through old, canceled checks. "Tell us again, did you hear anything? You live right below us. To make this much of a mess they would have had to have made some noise."

A startled sort of gasp escaped from the woman and, with it, she dropped a handful of papers back onto the floor.

"Damn," she said, stooping to pick them up. "I just remembered. I didn't hear anybody moving about up here. I did hear somebody knocking on the door for a long time though."

"Not so surprising," Jeremy said, putting Sheraton's computer disks back into a carton. "A burglar would have to be pretty damn sure that nobody was home before banging the door down."

"I thought that somebody was slamming their door shut," Pris explained, feeling all the worse for her mistake. "They do slam doors pretty badly in this building. They're all warped and never do shut properly by themselves."

"So, somebody knocked on the door and, after we didn't answer, they broke in and looked for... For what?" Jeremy felt a burning feeling of frustration and helplessness.

"They didn't only knock," Pris said. "The person called out your names also."

"You mean, you heard him-or was it a her-calling us?" Sheraton found the whole operation rather curious. Nothing, as far as he could see, was taken. Even a wristwatch that he cherished had only been shoved under the bed but not stolen.

"It was a he," Pris evasively answered.

"Who was it?" Jeremy felt familiar enough with this neighbor to get the suspicion that she was holding something back.

"That guy who was here the other night."

"You mean Mitch did this?" Jeremy angrily shouted.

"Not him," Pris said. "The other one. Jazz. The one who's a cross-dresser."

*   *   *

"Jazz," Sheraton said as patiently as he could. "This is important. We'd like to talk to you."

Sitting on the floor in front of the small white plastic and glass coffee table, Jazz was busily distributing various packets and cases of make-up in front of him making sure to leave enough room for the portable, two-sided mirror.

"I can listen to you and put on my war paint," he said as he squeezed dabs of color onto his fingertips and applied them to his cheeks with soft, round motions.

"Jazz," Jeremy said, having lost patience somewhere between the eye liner and the monumental debate Jazz had tried to embroil them into about which color lip gloss to use. "A lot is going on. You know more than you're telling any of us."

Mouth rounded in a round O shape, Jazz said: "A girl has got to keep some secrets or else the mystery is over."

"Your five o'clock shadow is the only secret you should be trying to keep hidden. This is serious. It's about Gene."

Although Jazz's long, dexterous fingers kept up a steady string of motions as they reached for various tubes, there was a contrived air about the whole process now.

"I can't talk about him," Jazz finally said, looking into the mirror as if to fix his lashes but trying to see Sheraton's face to judge it for his reaction.

"Jeremy and I lost track and got totally out of touch with Gene. What was Gene all about?" Sheraton asked him gently. "We knew him then. People change. What was Gene like before he died?"

"It's hard to think of him as dead," Jazz said.

"That's not an answer," Jeremy stormed. "It's a cop-out."

"There's this big air of mystery all about Gene," Sheraton explained. "What was he into? Jazz, what was he doing that could have caused somebody to want to kill him?"

"He was heavily into drugs," Jazz said, sounding as if he were using little effort in his speech. "Not only using them, but selling them."

"Gene was a pusher?" The thought of Gene as a drug dealer struck Sheraton immediately as preposterous. But, he had already admitted it; he and Jeremy had lost touch with the man. It was hard to tell what Gene might have been up to.

"It started with pot," Jazz explained. "Gene said it helped to alleviate the loneliness."

"Going out and having a social life would have been a lot better a way," Jeremy said angrily.

"Gene wasn't a social butterfly," Jazz reminded them. "He was a lot like you, Jeremy. He was shy and didn't know how to mingle."

"I'm shy but I'm not a drug addict," Jeremy said.

"He wasn't an addict," Jazz protested, putting down his eye brow pencil as if he had just been insulted. "I said he smoked grass."

"You said he started with pot. Naturally, there must have been a progression into other recreational drugs."

"Pills and cocaine. He mixed them with booze."

Jeremy sighed. "I'm surprised how he didn't kill himself if that was the trip he was on."

"He was into drugs," Sheraton said, trying not to be placement in his views on the subject. "How did he go from using drugs to selling them?"

"He got carried away," Jazz said, ignoring the make-up completely. "He really got into being stoned. He never got sick or hung-over so he never had a reason to stop and to dry out even though it got continually worse. He couldn't hold down a job."

"He was out of work?" Jeremy was surprised by this. "So he sold drugs to make a living and to keep himself in pot and coke?"

"It's also how he and I got reacquainted," Jazz said, softly choking back his tears. These tears were for himself; not for Gene. "Gene went on a drug trip and couldn't stop. I can relate to that. I don't do drugs. I guess Maybelline is my drug of choice if it has to come down to that. I got fired from jobs because even when I'm not dressed in drag, I'm still too lady-like to please some bosses. Those jobs where I could get work and not have an angry boss out to can me weren't any better. Then I had my co-workers harassing me.

"Gene and I met up again on the unemployment line. Both of us were about to have the government cut off our checks. We had pushed it to the limit. I was feeling really down and Gene was acting strange but friendly. I thought he was glad to see me and to become friends again. Only thing is, I didn't know that he wasn't glad to see me; he was so stoned that he would have struck up a friendship with a flag pole.

"We were both out of work with a lot of time on our hands. When Gene asked me to drop by and visit him, I thought that maybe God was finally giving me something I wanted."

Jazz quickly stopped speaking. He had gotten so carried away with his self-pity that he hadn't realized just how much he was revealing.

"You had a crush on Gene," Sheraton softly said. "There's nothing to be ashamed about in that."

"It was strictly platonic," Jazz insisted, sounding rueful enough so that both of his listeners knew that the platonic part of their relationship was Gene's decision.

Jazz looked at the sundry cosmetics lined out over the coffee table and began to try to finish his job on his face but his hands were trembling too much to do so.

"What else?" Jeremy asked him.

"Gene idolized the strangest people," Jazz said, speaking half to himself. "He thought that drug dealers were the coolest people."

"Of course," Jeremy said, surprising Sheraton with his insight. "A drug dealer is always going to suck up to his customers. Pay the man, take the crap he peddles and he'll call you his buddy."

"That was probably it," Jazz agreed. "Gene really worshipped those dudes. He wanted to be just like them."

"I have trouble thinking of anybody actually being envious of a man who stands in a school ground pushing drugs on small children," Sheraton shuddered.

"Gene didn't go that route," Jazz said indignantly. "He had morals and principles. He also had some wild ideas on how to make money selling dope."

"Were you involved in this?" Jeremy asked, trying not to come down too hard on the man. Through it all, it's always difficult to scream at somebody wearing blue eye shadow.

"Gene knew that the disco and party crowd were big drug buyers. He felt that there was a ready money market in selling to that crowd.

"Of course, if you knew anything about Gene, you'd know that he wouldn't set foot inside a gay bar or even a disco where straight and gay couples dance the night away."

"That's where you came in then."

"I loved going to dances and disco's," Jazz admitted freely. "I didn't want to sell drugs but—"

"But you felt that if you sold the drugs and handed the money over to Gene it would make him like you."

Jazz nodded and began to cry.

"Gene began to really get excited about my dressing up. I thought that maybe he was into guy's who put on ladies clothes and was interested.

"He didn't care about drag. What he did care about was the fact that drag costumes allowed a pusher a lot more leeway."

Sheraton and Jeremy exchanged a look between themselves and that at Jazz.

"I needed something to pad my bra with," Jazz rationalized. "It's a curse being born flat chested with today's look! Also, I never go anywhere without my bag of tricks." He tapped his ever ready purse. "After I used up my make-up-and I do use a lot of it-Gene had me save the tubes and such. He filled them with grass, pills and cocaine and I pushed the stuff for him."

"An ideal situation," Jeremy dryly said. "You did all the dirty work, could have gotten busted, and if you were hiding that stuff in your bra I mean it literally and figuratively, and Gene had only to sit at home getting stoned and wait for the night's earnings."

"It sounds that way when you say it," Jazz told him. "Gene made it sound like he was a CEO or financier. He had plans. He was going to become a drug king-pin. A really important man."

"So much for Gene's death," Jeremy said, rising. "I think you've explained that part of the story for us."

"No he didn't," Sheraton said, reminding Jeremy of a fact that had had been bothering him. He guessed that Jazz had come earlier, when he and Jeremy were taking their leisurely walk, probably just to bare his soul in hopes of clearing his conscious. But there was so much more, so many curious facts and pieces that didn't fit in. One thing that Gene's brother had mentioned to them right before he left struck a bell but Sheraton had been too tired and confused to question it then.

Sheraton turned to Jazz, took a tissue, and began to clean up his face.

"I guess I should start to invest in waterproof mascara."

"I think you should start acting like a responsible adult," Jeremy commented bitterly.

"Jazz," Sheraton said. "When you discovered Gene's body, what was he wearing?"

"Sheraton, I panicked and ran. I didn't check his wardrobe to see if his shirt matched his socks."

"He was in his underwear," Sheraton said. "Didn't that strike you as odd?"

"I don't remember that night," Jazz said, sounding honest and pained. "You're probably right but-"

"But Gene wasn't the sort of man to allow guest's over unless he had his shirt and pants on, isn't that right, Jazz?"

"You're right," Jazz said slowly. "Gene had a real phobia about things like that. He was always insisting that everybody was after him and trying to get into his pants. I guess I tried not to listen because I thought he knew the designs I was trying to draw on him. He never dressed up in a suit and tie but he wouldn't even wear shorts. He gave up food in favor of drugs. Gene was practically anorexia looking toward the end."

"The police report that was given to his family indicates that his sofa bed was open but not slept in and that Gene was wearing only a pair of underpants while his pants were on a chair right next to the bed."

"Gosh Sheraton, that is strange."

"Speaking of police reports," Jeremy added. "We had a visitor here recently. Know anything about it, Jazz?"

"Who was it?"

"Jazz," Sheraton said patiently. "Somebody broke in here and threw everything around looking for something. According to a witness, you were here that day looking for us."

"I didn't break in here," Jazz cried, standing up so quickly that he nearly knocked the coffee table over in the process.

"Why were you here?" Sheraton asked him.

"I had to tell you something," Jazz said and then stopped.

"Jazz, it's important that you tell us everything you know. Don't you see that Gene may have been killed by a drug dealer or by somebody who might know you?"

"I had a phone call," Jazz said in a rushed, strained voice. "I was to give you a message. I was to tell both you and Jeremy to stay away from Gene's friends and not to tell anything to the police."

"Who would have made such a phone call?" Sheraton asked.

"I don't know," Jazz said, crying again. "It scared me. I got worried about you. I even called your names when you didn't answer."

"Why would they have called up and said something like that?" Sheraton asked, half perplexed but half fascinated by the story. "Why and who?"

FIVE

It seemed that no matter how far down any given path they traveled, Jeremy and Sheraton were destined to come back to the starting zone.

After Jazz left, Jeremy's feelings about Sheraton's involvement with the death of Gene were reinforced. He felt that there were lies covering up other lies.

"'Smiling faces sometimes—'," he began to quote before Sheraton stopped him with: "Don't talk to me about song lyrics. This is serious, Jeremy."

"So is staying alive."

Jeremy might have found himself able to ignore Sheraton's furiously pounding information into a database. It was all a silly obsession, he thought, that would play itself out with time.

The appearance on their doorstep of two police detectives did nothing to either sweeten or brighten Jeremy's mood.

Detective Lawrence was a tall, solidly built man who was devoid of humor. He was filled with a sense of self-righteousness and had a rules and regulation booklet where his heart should have been. His partner, Detective Stone, was so enamored by Detective Lawrence that it was hard to hear what the great man had to say above and beyond Detective Stone's ass kissing noises.

"Pussycats," Detective Lawrence sneered, sitting down and spreading his legs far and wide. "I hear you two like to be where the action is."

"We're planning on selling tickets," Jeremy said, instantly disliking the man.

"Don't get mad at me, pussycat. I can't help it if trouble just seems to follow you *boy's* around," he said, crossing his leg so that a great expanse of shin showed. Strapped to his shin was a small pistol. "Let's see if a simple, slow, police officer can keep up with all the fun you've had up here recently.

"Now, a friend of yours died. Then there was a supposed break-in-"

"The door was knocked in," Sheraton explained. "You can check that out with the super."

"Your friend died and your front door was kicked in," Detective Stone said, taking up the thread. "What was stolen?"

"Nothing," Sheraton said, realizing how hollow it all sounded.

"Television, VCR, microwave oven-"

"My mother loves to send us gifts."

"Maybe you forgot to send her a thank-you note and your mother kicked your door in for you?"

Instead of being put out, Sheraton found it interesting.

"Then you think that the two incidents are related?"

Detective Lawrence looked at him strangely. "Pussycat, we're not paid to think."

"Then you really found your calling in life with this job," Jeremy grumbled.

"We're paid to ask questions," Detective Stone added sourly.

"So? Ask us a question."

"Why would somebody want to kick in your front door?" Detective Lawrence asked it as if there were a logical reason and it could be easily given to him.

"We don't know," Sheraton said. "They made a mess of things but, thank God, nothing else."

"The pussycat who died," Detective Lawrence said. "Somebody went through his pad too."

Neither Jeremy or Sheraton had known that. Jeremy didn't necessarily believe it either.

"What did they take from Gene?" Sheraton asked.

"He didn't file a report," Detective Stone guffawed.

"People are murdered every day," Jeremy said, suddenly understanding-judging by the police force exhibit in front of him-why that was possible. "People are also robbed and their homes are broken into regularly. The two don't necessarily go together."

"They do if the robbery was caused to retrieve something that might have been the property of the murder victim," Detective Lawrence grinned.

Sheraton waved his hands wildly. "We hadn't seen Gene in months. Why, I doubt if you'd even find an old Christmas card here from him."

"When a pusher dies, it's not Christmas cards that robbers are after," Detective Stone said too seriously to be believed.

"How about drugs?" Detective Lawrence asked. "You pussycats like candy?"

"I'm on a diet and Sheraton is practically a diabetic," Jeremy said flatly.

Detective Lawrence cocked his head to one side. "People with a fat ass always claim they're dieting. And, what's with this diabetic crap? A convenient excuse to explain some of your buddy's needle marks?"

"It was a joke," Sheraton explained, feeling almost compelled to show his arms at this point. "You can't seriously think that we were buying drugs from Gene! Besides, we were the ones who were robbed."

"Which would only mean that somebody may have ripped you off after you iced that other pussycat and ripped him off," Detective Lawrence explained. "Look. Me and my partner don't give a damn what you shove up your noses or your ass holes."

"Who gives you those inspirational thoughts?" Jeremy asked. "Norman Vincent Peale?"

"We care about justice," Detective Stone exclaimed. Jeremy waited for him to pull out a badge and gaze at it lovingly.

"Then find out who killed Gene and who broke into our place," Jeremy said dryly.

Detective Lawrence stared at his partner for a long time and then winked maliciously. From within his breast coat pocket, he pulled out a glassine envelope.

"Look familiar, pussycats?" he asked as he waved it high up in the air above their heads.

"Never seen it before," Jeremy said hastily. He knew what the bag contained.

"A lot of cocaine in this bag," the officer said with a snide expression on his face. "And guess where we found this, pussycats?"

"In Gene's apartment," Jeremy said, not realizing that he was playing into the man's hands.

"Wrong guess," Detective Stone laughed. "How about you, blondie? Want to try your luck?"

Sheraton didn't have to guess. He didn't believe it but he found himself filled with a dreadful fear all the same.

"Right here," Detective Lawrence said, still waving the bag. "Our man who came when you called in your report found this lying all sweet and cozy just waiting for some stupid flat foot to discover."

"Do you think if we had an opium den here that we'd have called the police?" Jeremy screamed.

"But, you didn't call the police," Detective Lawrence said, aping Jeremy's voice. "A neighbor called the cops. Probably some dummy who didn't know how bad you boy's were."

"Or," Detective Stone added. "A neighbor who knew and wanted to get you out of this respectable building."

"Perverts," Detective Lawrence proclaimed. "Or don't you think I don't know just what kind of pussycats you are and what kind of cream you're both after?"

"Being you're so into animals, I suppose you'll tell us that a little birdie told you that," Jeremy said.

"I'm only trying to be your friend," Detective Lawrence told them. "You play with me and I'll play with you."

"He's right, Sheraton. I already feel like we're both being diddled."

"Cut the shit," Detective Stone screamed, looking at Detective Lawrence to see if he had said it correctly. "Answer us when we talk to you."

"You haven't talked to us," Sheraton said. "You've made wild accusations. None of them happen to be true."

"And this wonderful Brazilian export isn't yours?" Detective Lawrence looked as if he were going to go back into his pocket, retrieve the cocaine, and wave it around again.

Suddenly, inspiration hit Jeremy. "Does it have our fingerprints on it?"

Detective Lawrence and Detective Stone tried to look smug but the air had leaked out of their balloon.

"So then you deny owning an illegal substance?" Detective Stone asked, seriously.

"We deny it emphatically," Sheraton assured him.

"Then let me congratulate you, pussycats." Detective Lawrence looked even angrier now. "You're the only people alive who ever had a break-in and, instead of being robbed, had the robber leave you a little present."

"Sort of makes you wonder what it's like here on Christmas morning," Jeremy smiled.

"Maybe I'll stick around and just find out for myself," Detective Lawrence said, rising. "Don't think that either of you pussycats has seen the last of me."

*   *   *

- 56 -

Jeremy was a very determined man who was beginning to feel the stirring's of impatience ruling over him as a predominating factor.

He was determined-usually quite loudly-that Sheraton should poke his nose out of the events.

"Even with us standing on the side lines," Sheraton replied. "We still are being pushed into the middle of things."

Pris sat and listened to the semi-quarrel and found herself strangely placed somewhere in the middle. She believed that Jeremy had a logical theory or two involved in his decision to play it safe and steer clear of the murder investigation.

Sheraton, she also felt, was campaigning a private crusade all his own. It wasn't a game-she couldn't quite picture him as one who amused himself in such a way. He was a man who stood by his friends-no matter where the past had lead their friendship to-and was willing to go out on any limb for them. He wanted to save their reputations.

Or, in Gene's case, their memory.

Jeremy was stoic in his firmness. Sheraton could be rather impassive. It wasn't a heated argument; more of a dead-lock between sides.

It was Marty and Karen who managed to tilt things in favor of Sheraton's determination to keep himself firmly involved in the midst of things.

"It's a beautiful afternoon," Sheraton said into the phone when they called. "What are you doing?"

"Trying hard to cope with diaper rash, little Marty's cold and big Marty's depression," Karen said, sounding equally heartless and indifferent to all concerned.

"What's the matter?" Sheraton asked Marty who had picked up the extension.

"It's just a feeling that we've finally gotten old," Marty said quickly-too quickly Sheraton felt. "Has all this gotten to you and Jeremy too?"

"It's difficult," Sheraton admitted, trying to console his friend by commiserating with him. "You expect these sort of things to happen in books or silly movies. Somehow, you never think of real people dying."

"Not in that way," Marty agreed in a voice lacking any true conviction.

"I told him we should pack up the kids and go visit my mother," Karen said, her voice blasting over the wire. "We have that beautiful new car and I washed my hair just last week so I'm all set to go. Only Marty acts like he won't be having fun if we go to visit mother."

Both Jeremy and Sheraton had met Karen's mother. Jeremy likened the woman to motherhood's answer to the Hindenberg disaster. She had a tongue about as salty as Ruth's must have been after God had turned her into a pillar. It was clear that, if you were feeling blue, she wouldn't be the logical choice for cheering up Marty.

"How about if you go and see your mother and I head downtown and visit with Sheraton and Jeremy?" Marty asked.

Sheraton had to sit holding the phone several inches away from his ear as Karen told Marty her opinion about that.

It was a near certainty in Sheraton's mind that Marty had carefully planned to pop this question to his wife when Sheraton was on the phone. Karen argued that Marty had too much fun in his life. She cited examples of riding the subways at rush hour and hasty lunches at his office desk as prime examples of all the fun that Marty had every work day.

Finally, in a huffy voice, she consented to let Marty visit them without her.

"Don't worry about me," she said in a flat voice of anger. "I'll find something to do while you're out gallivanting around with your friends."

Sheraton could almost have chuckled about the spat except that, when he told Jeremy of Marty's impending visit, he found himself with his own lover's quarrel on his hands.

"I'm not really in the mood to see anyone," Jeremy said, pulling the *Sunday Times* up around his nose.

This act didn't deter Sheraton.

"Then how about you staying here and Marty and I will go to brunch?"

Jeremy was on the point of agreeing when he back-tracked.

"What are you up to now?" he asked doubtfully.

"Marty's feeling a bit down and I—"

"And you see this as a perfect opportunity to find out more about Gene and snoop. Sheraton, I don't want us involved in any of this. Wasn't that scene with that awful Detective Lawrence enough to turn you sour on the whole thing?"

"Suppose Detective Lawrence came down just as hard on Marty as he did on us? Don't you think that Marty-who is a sensitive guy-feels just as bad as we do now?"

"I can't see Detective Lawrence or anybody getting the best of Karen," Jeremy said. "After all, the man only had a gun and a license to kill. He wasn't prepared to battle the likes of Karen Sanders."

"All the same," Sheraton said as he slipped a fresh polo shirt over his head. "Marty is depressed and maybe this will cheer him up."

"And you're not going to try your hand at snooping or solving this murder case?"

"I think I'll try taking him to that little place on Hudson Street for lunch," Sheraton continued. "You don't think it will turn him off because it's gay, do you?"

Jeremy snapped the fresh paper in his hands. "Sheraton, you will stay out of the murder investigation."

"Sure you don't want to join us?" Sheraton asked as he went out the door to wait for Marty in front of the building.

*   *   *

"You don't mind the fact that your lover is going out with another man?" Pris asked Jeremy, half-seriously but balancing the question with enough dead panned humor to make it sound fluffy.

Jeremy looked at the woman. It was hard for him to think of Pris as someone who he and Sheraton had just met. She had an abrasive, almost caustic tongue but she channeled it into a dry, biting wit that suited Jeremy's style just fine.

"Hush puppies, double knit slacks and he still thinks that mousse is a French dessert. If Sheraton were to leave me for Marty I wouldn't sue for alienation of affection; I'd have him declared insane."

"Your friends certainly don't spend much time reading *Gentlemen's Quarterly*." Pris' outfit-jeans with the legs pulled up to a mid-calf length and a ratty looking T-shirt-seemed to make her observation even funnier than she had meant it to be.

"You're thinking of Mitch."

"I try not to do that-ever."

"Then you're a female chauvinist," Jeremy teased her. "I notice how quick you are to put down the male species but how is it that both Barbara and Karen escaped your fashion-conscious observation?"

"I didn't even notice them," Pris said. "I *heard* the both of them and, believe me, that was more than enough."

"I suppose that, to the uninitiated, we are an odd, little group."

"Walking right into a scene like the one I stumbled into, it would be only natural to think that. A drag queen passed out on your sofa. A woman who dresses like a drag queen walking around and screaming as if she were a blood clot wearing a veiled hat."

"And then we come to darling Karen," Jeremy wryly observed.

"I'm sure she's just a prisoner of domestic bliss," Pris responded. "Too bad she's just not a prisoner and let domestic bliss be damned."

"I don't dislike Karen," Jeremy said. "Well, not exactly. She just has this habit of getting on one's nerves at every moment."

"She's terribly vocal and extremely critical."

Pris nodded. "I saw a guy wearing a shirt that said, 'Life's a bitch and then you marry one'. I think your pal Karen was the inspiration for that little ditty."

"I don't think that either Sheraton or I ever took the time to seriously consider Karen," Jeremy said.

"Why would anybody spend their time thinking of her?"

"Today she's got Sheraton's mind working overtime."

"He's really intent on solving this case and finding out who killed your friend, isn't he?"

Jeremy looked momentarily as if he were about to explode.

"It must be a quaint, mid-western custom. I don't think they have arcade games in dairy states."

"You're a lot like me," Pris said. "You don't get involved." There was a pause that only Jeremy assumed was natural and not staged. "At least, you don't get involved in things until they strike too close to home."

"You think that I should join ranks with Sheraton and become one of the Hardy Boys?"

"I don't know if you should," Pris explained. "I just know that, like it or not, you've been tossed into the pot with the rest of this mess."

Reflecting upon her words, Jeremy found it hard to deny some of Pris' points. He was concerned and very upset. Much of what he resented about Sheraton's investigating the murder stemmed out of fear. Fear and fact. He wondered if Sheraton had ever stopped to realize that he wasn't capable of defending himself against a killer.

"Want me to get that?" Pris asked as a loud series of bangs were exalted upon the door.

"Logically, I should say, 'No' and be done with it," Jeremy sighed. "It can only be more trouble."

Pris laughed but rose to answer the door. She found Jeremy to be a pessimist and was seriously hoping to prove him wrong.

"Who," Karen said sharply, "are you?"

Pris opened the door wider and was momentarily stumped for an answer.

"We met the other night," she said, fighting the urge to put the visitor in her place. "It was a bit of a madhouse here and perhaps you've forgotten."

"Is Jeremy Baker home?" Karen didn't wait for an answer for, as she spoke she barged into the room.

"Karen," Jeremy exclaimed, surprised both to see the woman and not to see her husband trailing in her wake. "This is a surprise."

"I hope I'm not interrupting anything," Karen said bitterly, looking at Pris as if she had just discovered her long, lost nemesis. "I had a hell of a time finding a baby sitter on such short notice. I'd hate to think of all my time and money being wasted."

"I was just leaving," Pris said, slapping a happy smile on her face while she shot Jeremy a cynical look.

"Oh, must you?" Jeremy asked, suddenly finding himself feeling a slight bit nervous.

"Yeah," Karen sharply yipped. "She must. Me and you have many important things to talk about, Jeremy."

"Then I really should be going," Pris said sweetly to Karen. Turning to Jeremy, she added: "I'd hate to interrupt anything important."

After she had left, Karen continued to just glare at Jeremy as if they had been in the midst of a discussion that should have automatically been resumed at this point.

"Does Marty know you're here?" Jeremy finally asked, too confused to offer her anything more than a question.

"No he does not. And don't you go running off and ratting me out. Not even to Sheraton."

"Why all the clandestineness?"

"Don't use those big words, Jeremy. We're not in college anymore."

"What the fuck are you doing here?"

"Can't an old friend drop by?" Karen huffed, sounding slightly insulted.

Jeremy looked at her and then taunted himself into looking at Karen with Sheraton's eyes.

She had dressed hastily. Her blouse was half pulled out of her pants and her shoes were scuffed and not the sort that she would normally wear on the street.

But what, Jeremy wondered, precipitated (er, caused) her to leave home so quickly that she hadn't bothered to change her clothes first?

"Marty and Sheraton are out having fun," she said, sitting down opposite Jeremy. She spread her legs defiantly and looked in the mood for a good, long fight. "Who cares about you and me, right Jeremy?"

"Sheraton left here with my blessings," Jeremy told Karen. (And also my American Express card to help pay for brunch.)

"I suppose the big boy's have many important things they have to talk about when we're not around," Karen replied. (Why the hell doesn't anybody ever treat me to a free meal?)

Jeremy smiled wanly. "It's all proper and innocent." (I'll kill Sheraton if it isn't.)

"Yes," Karen evenly replied. "I'm sure it is proper and innocent." (I'll kill Sheraton if it isn't.)

Karen opened up her pocketbook and retrieved her cigarettes. She lit one and then carelessly threw the match on the coffee table top.

"Barbara's gone too damn far this time," she said through a mouthful of smoke. "Why the hell doesn't she leave us all alone?"

"What has Our-Lady-Of-The-Shock-Treatments done this time?"

"Talking to the police," Karen yelled. "Filling their heads with all sorts of wild ideas about Gene's death."

"Wasn't it Shakespeare who wrote something about being told by an idiot?"

"She's just crazy enough to make the cops believe some of the wild lies she's telling," Karen complained viciously. "Let's face it, men are fools."

Jeremy nodded. "You're talking to somebody who owns one."

Karen's eyes flashed. "What? Oh. Don't let's talk about that."

"Right," Jeremy agreed. "What should we talk about instead?"

"You like the fact that the cops are hounding the living daylights out of us because of that bitch Barbara?"

"Hardly. I just don't think they're operating under her instructions."

"Where do you think they're getting half their crazy ideas from then?" Karen forgot the cigarette smoldering in the ashtray and lit a fresh one. "Barbara's actually got the police believing that she was Gene's lover and that he confided in her."

"Maybe he and Barbara did have a thing," Jeremy said.

"Get real!" Karen was in a flying rage of fury now. "Gene hated her-that's probably the wisest thing Gene ever did. He couldn't stand Barbara and she hated him too. Have you noticed that all this, 'The man I loved' business didn't start until *after* Gene died?"

Jeremy was feeling the burnt out ends of a very long week causing him to be extremely short.

"In the long run, what does it matter? Barbara is lying and she can't hurt us?"

"Suppose she knows things that could hurt all of us?" Karen said the words so wildly that Jeremy became immediately interested.

"What could Barbara know?"

"Suppose she and Gene did have a thing going between them?"

"You're the one who just said he couldn't stand her and vice-versa."

"Suppose they had a friendship of sorts," Karen said. "Suppose in a weak moment Gene told that skank something that could hurt some of us now?"

"What could he have told Barbara?"

"Suppose he told Barbara that he and I were lovers," Karen said bitterly.

"But that's ridiculous," Jeremy said to her. Karen, he felt, could be a lot of things-starting with being a bitch-but unfaithful to Marty just wasn't in her repertoire.

"Is it?" Karen asked him. "Is it really crazy, Jeremy? Suppose I were to tell you it was true? What would you say then?"

"I'd ask you if it were true."

Slowly, not looking at him, Karen announced: "It was true. It's all true."

SIX

Put Marty in a dressy suit and he would look unruffled and coarse. Dressed in a leisurely way, he seemed as if he had just been unrolled out of a bed.

Sheraton and Marty walked a few blocks and enjoyed some sunshine and coolish weather. Both commented rapidly and steadily on such. Both had a lot to talk about but there seemed no available foot hold to begin.

Sitting down in a milestone gay restaurant (at least in the way of longevity as it had been under the same management team for almost a year), Sheraton first wondered if being in a predominantly gay eatery would upset Marty. When a few minutes had passed and Marty still hadn't commented on the fact that the room was crowded up to the rafters but only with men, Sheraton realized that there was something weighing so heavily on Marty's mind that, in turn, he didn't notice where he was.

Folding his hands on the scarred, slightly wobbly wooden table, Sheraton let Marty know that he was there for him.

"Thanks," Marty said, casting aside a menu that he hadn't glanced at although he held it for a long enough period. "It's this business with Gene."

"It's got all of us down," Sheraton commiserated. "Perhaps a glass of wine?"

"Huh?" Marty was so freely drifting in and out of a dream world that he was hardly paying attention. It wasn't until the waiter approached the table and said, "What will you girls have?" that anything operating on a level outside his mind began to effect him.

"What did he call us?" Marty asked, reaching for the menu and using it almost as a shield.

"It's an old joke."

"Sorry." Marty forced a smile on his face. "I'm just too caught up in all this mess to be thinking straight." He made a motion of slapping his hand over his mouth. "I shouldn't have said that."

Not that many opportunities, Sheraton knew, come in this life so he generally made the most of the meager ones that came his way.

"Instead of minding your social p's and q's, how about telling me all about what's got you so upset?"

Marty paused while the waiter hastily dropped a carafe of red wine on the table.

"Like I told you, it's about Gene's death."

"It's on all our minds, Marty. The thing is to try and get over it."

"I'm trying," a worried Marty admitted. He poured a glass of wine, held the glass up as if to toast Sheraton and then lost all interest.

"What did you think about Gene?" Marty asked the question in a deliberately open-ended way. As men in plaid work shirts jostled about their table, Sheraton tried to figure out which of the many avenues Marty wanted him to go down with for the answer.

"Jeremy and I lost touch with Gene. You know that."

"I mean, what did you think of him before you broke it off the friendship? What did you feel about Gene? What did you know about Gene?"

Sheraton begged for a moment to collect his thoughts, ordered a salad nicose and waited until the waiter delivered their brunch before speaking.

"Jeremy felt that he got a vicarious thrill out of saying things that would upset people."

Marty looked up from a black olive that he was studying so intently that it almost worried Sheraton.

"Vicarious thrill or vicious thrill?"

"You know Jeremy," Sheraton said. "He wasn't too keen on Gene after we came out of the closet to him.

"I know that it must have been a difficult time for Gene as he might not have been fully prepared to accept our gayness but-"

"But Gene flipped out totally and did everything he could to blast both you and Jeremy to hell." Marty seemed to find a guided relief in the confession. "There are some things you don't talk about; the way Gene treated you guy's is a prime example.

"He bad mouthed you to everyone. It was your privilege and your right to tell whomever you pleased that you were…this way. After you confessed to Gene, he did everything but put an ad in the paper announcing the fact."

"It really didn't matter," Sheraton said seriously.

"His telling everybody might not have mattered: the way he tried to hurt you both was very wrong. He didn't tell people that you were homosexuals because he had trouble accepting the fact that you were. He told them because he wanted to hurt you."

"He didn't."

"Not for a lack of trying," Marty said. "He called everybody up and said something like, 'You certainly can't be *their* friend any longer. They're sick.'. It was disgusting."

"You and Karen are still our friends. He might have tried but he didn't hurt us," Sheraton said, wondering how much Gene had actually hurt himself. "It was also a long time ago, Marty. Why bring that incident up now?"

"Homosexuality was a big thing to Gene. Some people still walk up to you and say, 'What's your sign?' but in Gene's case it was always, 'Are you queer?'. You had to notice his obsession with the topic. It was all he ever talked and bitched about to anyone he met."

"I assume that you were one of the candidates who had to continually listen to Gene's views on gay's."

Men popped tabs on frosty cans of beer. In the blue darkness, laughter erupted. Secrets and stories were being shared. But all that Sheraton could see was a deep, troubled line twisting Marty's mouth.

"Marty," Sheraton finally said. "Something's playing heavy on your mind. What is it?"

"You know I work over at the newspaper. It's a good job but it's tough. The pay is OK but Karen makes many demands on me. Oh, she means well. It's always for the kids. It's a bit muddled to me how her mink coat was actually helping our kids education but … Still, it's a big drain and it keeps on becoming an even bigger responsibility for me.

"Back in college, when we talked about getting married, we thought it would be going out to dinners, holding hands and having fun while trying to make ends meet. Well, we try to make the ends meet but it isn't very much fun."

"Jeremy envisioned us as growing old together while we listened to his old *Crosby, Stills & Nash* albums on the record player," Sheraton admitted as he unfolded his napkin. "Whoever would have thought that when Jeremy purchased his record player way back then he was buying a potential artifact?"

Marty gave him a small grin. "Things change. The trouble is, they never seem to change for the better, do they?

"Every week, it's the same story. No matter how much overtime I put in, there's never enough money to pay all the bills. Karen always feels the kids need more or that we have to replace something that broke."

"Jeremy and I are fortunate," Sheraton said. "We have two pay checks coming in every week." He wondered if he should be more direct in his meaning.

"Karen won't work," Marty answered, taking the implication. "She's cooped up all day with the kids and has little time to herself. She thinks that when I go to work at least I get to be in the outside world and meet people and see things. She has nothing but the kids and the laundry. I'm not complaining about Karen. It's hard for her."

Sympathetically, Sheraton answered: "It's difficult for both of you."

"I feel that I have no life. There's nothing but work at nine, home to hear the complaints and then back to work again. Maybe you and Jeremy had the right idea. You're together but you still have your separate identities. Somewhere along the line, I seem to have lost mine."

Sheraton moved some black olives around his plate. He was sure there was more to the story than this. There was.

"At work, I met up with some people who are good people. They're bright and they're funny." Marty now pushed away his uneaten omelet. He couldn't pretend any more. "I became pretty close to one of them."

"Karen doesn't like that?"

"Karen doesn't know about it," Marty replied. "We don't do anything to be ashamed of; we just laugh. That's what's missing from my life-laughter.

"I suppose you know that Gene couldn't hold down a job or, if he persuaded somebody to hire him, he couldn't keep the job. He had a bucolic temper."

"A side-effect of the drugs?"

"Probably. Any way, he was always in the poor house. I tried to help him out. I slipped him a few bucks. Believe me, it wasn't easy for me to do that."

"I suppose that, with your children, every penny really does count."

"With Karen it's me who has to account for every penny. She studies every pay voucher as if she were going to be quizzed on it. She noticed that I was holding back some money but I managed to fancy dance my way out of that one."

"How much money did Gene ask you for, Marty?"

A red blush crept up Marty's face.

"A lot," he said in a barely audible voice.

"How could you give Gene large sums of money if Karen handles the family finances and guards them?"

"I had a small savings account-a couple of thousand dollars-back from when I was a kid. I closed the account and gave the money to Gene. Karen didn't even know I had that money."

Sheraton suspected that Marty was telling the truth but leaving out much the story.

"Did Gene tell you what he needed the money for?"

Marty shook his head. If possible, he even looked more worried now.

"It was very kind of you to help him out," Sheraton said, wondering if Marty would tell him any more. "I'm sure that, with his drug habit and not being able to hold down a job, that money came in handy."

"I didn't give him the money because I wanted him to buy drugs with it and keep himself perpetually stoned." Although Marty's voice was loud, it was hardly raised in anger; he was trying to explain something he had never wanted to talk about.

"I know that. Why did you give him so much money?"

"That friend from the paper I was telling you about...Sheraton, he's gay."

"Don't say it as if I might know him," Sheraton smiled. "Believe it or not, there are still a few gay's in the city who Jeremy and I haven't met."

"Gene was hounding me for money," Marty continued, speaking as if he never heard Sheraton. "Even after I gave him all that money, he kept coming back and demanding more and more. I didn't have it to give him."

"Surely he understood that."

"Gene didn't want to understand anything. He wanted money."

Sheraton was beginning to see an image-still blurry-forming in the tale.

"Gene found a way to try and get more money from you, didn't he Marty?"

Marty bit his lip. "Yeah. He never was bold enough to go up to our apartment when he tried to bilk me for more money. He met me downstairs-at first. Then he began to wait for me outside the building where I work. That's when it happened."

"What?"

Marty looked as if he were going to be sick. "He followed me and my friend one night. He followed us to a bar." There was a long pause which Marty punctuated heavily with eye contact. "I guess you can suspect what sort of bar."

"Anybody can go into a gay bar," Sheraton firmly stated. "It doesn't mean a thing."

"Maybe to you and me it doesn't mean squat. Can you imagine what Gene made out of it?"

"Marty, I'm sure it was perfectly innocent."

"Some of the guy's who hung out in the bar knew me by sight. We joked and kidded with one another. Gene hid in one corner of the bar when he followed me there-why do they keep those bars so dark?-and he saw things that could be easily misconstrued."

Sheraton grasped it all in. Suddenly his salad held no appeal to him. As voices on this lazy Sunday grew friendlier and the laughter louder, he felt a burning disenchantment growing like a wild fire within him. "And Gene threatened to tell Karen about your visit and your friends at the gay bar."

Marty nodded. "With Karen, it doesn't matter if you're guilty or not. Once she has an idea-though it's unproved-in her head, it's hard to convince her otherwise."

Sheraton was all too sure of that.

"Gene really began to put the screws to me. He said that he had a camera and that he took pictures. That was all I needed. He said that first he'd show them to Karen and then to my boss. Either way you look at it, I would have been in the dog house.

"I went to my parents and gave them some song-and-dance number and they gave me the money Gene was demanding."

"Did you give it to Gene?"

"No." There was a lusterless, thudding tone in his voice. "I was suppose to give it to Gene that night."

"The night he was killed?"

"Sounds like something straight out of a movie, doesn't it?"

"You went to Gene's apartment to give him the money?" Sheraton felt his pulse racing but his mind was crystal clear and sharp now.

"I went there. Of course, there was no answer when I knocked. I don't know why but I tried the door. It was open."

"Dear God," Sheraton exclaimed.

"I ran," Marty said, sobbing freely now. "I was so scared that I ran away. That's why Jazz found the door open when he went. I ran so fast I forgot to close it."

"Did anybody see you?" Sheraton asked.

"I don't know," Marty said, wiping tears away with his napkin. "I thought nobody did. Now I'm not so sure."

"Why?"

"Barbara," Marty said. "She called me at work. I thought she was lying about how close she and Gene were. Now I'm not so sure. She knows things."

"What things?" Sheraton asked, keeping his voice level. His lunch was now forgotten. As nice as the day had felt when it started, there was a dismal gloom rapidly falling on him now. How little he knew about his friends.

"She's only hinting but she knows something, Sheraton. I don't know what but she knows something. Maybe she has those photos of me."

"Marty," Sheraton said, suddenly having to admit to himself that he was stumbled and fuddled enough not to know where to go. "I don't know what to say."

"I'm scared," Marty sniffed. "Barbara has the police looking for a killer and she's going to tell them it's me. I know it, Sheraton. I just know it."

*   *   *

"Let's face it, the thrill has gone out of my marriage."

Karen walked around the small living room, flailing her arms around her and moving with quick, jerky steps.

Jeremy listened to her but he found the whole performance of body language to be a much more telling story.

Karen's eyes were darting around the room in furious circles, she never looked at him. Even when she walked, she seemed set on some sort of automatic pilot control that kept her clear out of his path. The blatancy of her confession didn't succeed totally because Karen seemed to be holding back almost as much as she was giving.

"You and Gene had an affair," Jeremy said, wondering how Karen would react to the word.

"I was bored; half out of my mind from loneliness. Do you realize that it's been years since I had an intelligent conversation with someone who didn't have pabulum on their breath?"

"So Gene was a great conversationalist."

Karen looked at Jeremy to see if she could figure out how much he believed and just how much he was going to ride her.

"I'm not saying that I was in love with him. Gene was too weird for me."

"Let's leave love and stimulating conversations in the afternoon out of this," Jeremy said, suddenly drawn into the conversation although he wasn't sure why. "How were you able to cope with Gene's problem?"

It surprised Jeremy that Karen didn't falter or even make a pretense at not understanding.

"The drugs? Hey, that was his thing. What did I care?"

"He was going a little bit too far over the edge by all reports."

"Reports?" Karen's normally harsh voice was now choppy. "You mean that's what Jazz told you. You can't believe a thing that man says. I think smelling all that nail polish remover finally got to him.

"Gene did drugs. So what? Weren't we children once as well?"

"That doesn't mean that we still all have black lights burning while we listen to protest songs."

Looking as if she were a tiger set to pounce upon a victim, Karen stood with her arms akimbo as she spoke. "Are you trying to say that you think I was mixed up with drugs too?"

"Were you?" Jeremy didn't wait for an answer. "You're the one who told me that you were bored and lonely. Also, you made no bones about the fact that Gene wasn't romantic or a great lover."

"I don't take drugs," she said calmly. She ran her hands down the side of her blouse as if finding her hands had suddenly grown to clumsy for her to balance. "He did and it wasn't my place to stop him."

"Gene's drug infatuation is rather interesting."

Karen seemed to believe that Jeremy wasn't accusing her of being a user but she remained guarded and edgy.

"What," she asked, "did Jazz tell you?"

"Gene didn't stop with just taking a fit hits off a lid. He was pushing the stuff as well."

A deflated woman sat on the sofa and, for the moment, much of the life seemed to have been sucked out of her.

"Life's boring," she finally said, speaking as if she were an Atlas who could no longer carry his weight. "Marty's sweet and all that but it's just not fun. Truthfully, it never was."

"Watching Gene get stoned or standing around while he pushed coke was a quick pick-me-up?"

"You guy's have your fun," Karen screamed, her voice strident and piercing. "You don't have the responsibilities and the obligations that I'm saddled down with everyday. Even if we could afford the baby-sitters, I still can't get Marty off that sofa at nights. The most exciting thing that ever happens to me is when they interrupt *Days Of Our Lives* for a special bulletin."

"I'm still young. I've still got life left in me. Sure Gene wasn't a great romancer. Of course he was conceited and strange. He was mean too. But he also introduced me to the sort of life where there is some exhilaration. He had his drug and I had mine-danger.

"Sneaking around, hoping that nobody would see me entering or leaving his apartment, that was all exciting. Even when he started talking about me peddling the drugs, it wasn't quite so crazy sounding after I got use to the idea. There was a definite risk involved but, in a satirical sort of way, it was fun."

"Gene wanted you to push dope?" Jeremy found this incredulous to accept.

"He felt that I wasn't the only bored housewife in town and, he was right. There are other girls I know who are pulled out of the real world and reduced to living in a state where the shine on the kitchen floor is the only important thing that will ever happen to them. He felt that there was a good market there."

"Wasn't he the entrepreneur."

Karen slapped a burnt match into the ash tray. "Think about it, Baker. It's not such a totally screwed up idea."

"So you became the candy man for the all the bored-with-life little ladies who you meet at the school play groups?"

Karen sat up straight and looked as if she were slightly proud of the fact. Then, when it came time to orally agree, she lost some demeanor of arrogance.

"I didn't like the idea any more than you did. It was an exciting thought-I didn't lie to you about that. But, I wasn't going to do it just because I thought it would be a great help to the other women in my position. I did it to get Gene to like me."

"Why would Gene's liking you be so important that you were willing to become a pusher to get his approval?"

"Normally, I'd say that as a man you wouldn't understand. Perhaps, in your case, you would.

"He didn't want me-not in the lover and mistress role. He played the part of the faithful servant. Sweet talked me and told me how much he cared for me. But, he only said those things and acted that way when I agreed to push his shit for him.

"He was so damn smug and so confident. I don't know if he was really having it off with Barbara. He acted satisfied enough so that he must have been getting it from somebody. For all I knew, it could even have been from Jazz. At first I didn't care.

"At first, if you want the whole, filthy story, I didn't want Gene as my lover. It was just the mystery of the whole thing that eventually got to me. He saw that I was interested and he used it. He didn't use it to get sex: he used it as an opportunity for himself."

"How long did this relationship between the two of you continue?"

Karen seemed nervous now.

"It went on for some time."

Jeremy knew that she was holding back something just as he knew that it was something important.

"Karen, did you ever end your relationship-business or otherwise-with Gene or did it continue until the day he was murdered?"

"You're not implying that I killed him, are you?"

"I'm asking a different question altogether."

Karen sank back in the sofa, lit a fresh cigarette, and moaned. "I was suppose to have made a major drug sale the day Jazz discovered his body. I had the stuff in my purse and I was suppose to push it to my Mah Jong club. That's what I told Gene I was going to do. Of course, I couldn't.

"I've been fudging the budget. Marty doesn't know or suspect. I took the grass from Gene and paid him for it out of my pocket. I told him I was selling it to a girl friend when I was really flushing it down the toilet. It always made him so happy, and he always treated me so damn great, that I got carried away with the whole thing.

"The last time, he really insisted that I had to start going all the way. He didn't want to hear about how scared I was. He insisted that it had to be cocaine-not just grass-and a large amount of it too.

"Of course I protested. I raised a holy stink. I can do that you know."

Jeremy nodded his head. He had no problem in believing that Karen could cause a fuss.

"He got adamant about it," Karen continued. "He said that if we could make this major sale, things would turn around for him and he'd have more money to spend on us. That was something I hadn't expected. He made it sound like we could stop the slap-and-tickle routine and get into the real stuff."

Jeremy stared at her but tried to be non-committal. "So, with the promise that, when you returned with the money in hand and left the ladies of your club with buzzing noses, Gene would deflower you, you pretended to go along with the scheme?"

"I took the cocaine he pushed on me," Karen said. "He had a way about him when it came to drugs. It was hard to say no to him."

"But you took the drugs?"

"Yeah. I took them. Don't you see, Jeremy, I had to take them and promise to sell them?"

"You had to put yourself in a position where you could have gotten arrested on a felony-not to mention having Mah Jong tiles thrown at you-so you could have had a roll in the hay with Gene?"

"He became a lot more forceful than that," Karen said, lowering her voice and speaking in a tone that Jeremy didn't recognize coming from her-normal and not abrasive.

"He would have told Marty what he and I were up to," she said. "Even though we still hadn't gone all the way, it would have put me in a lot of hot water. Marty's mother doesn't like me-impossible as that might sound."

"He threatened to blackmail you?"

"After I had the chance to think it over, that's exactly what he did. I didn't realize it at first. I took the cocaine but I couldn't go through with selling it. It wasn't only because I was scared or that I couldn't squeeze enough money out of the household funds that I didn't sell the stuff. It was because Gene had finally pushed me too far and I was disgusted.

"I went to his place right before Marty came home from work. I was going to throw the shit in his face and read Gene the riot act while I was at it. I figured that if he tried to hurt me, I could hurt him too by having him busted."

"Was he dead when you got there?" Jeremy asked.

"No," Karen said, surprising him. "He was there and I gave him back the cocaine and told him where he could put it-and I didn't mean his nose either. He took it and argued with me. We got into a fight but it was a real quick fight. He pushed me out of the place after a few minutes."

"How many minutes, Karen?"

"Less than five," she answered. "He and I had one hell of an argument but then he kicked me out. He was alive when I left."

"Did you go back later?"

"How did you know that?" Karen screamed.

"You've told me all this, why not come clean and tell me the rest," Jeremy suggested.

"I forgot my pocketbook there," Karen said. "I didn't realize it until I got home. I would have left it there but for two reasons.

"First, I didn't want Gene to have any evidence to show to my husband. Secondly, I had all my money in the purse. For a crazy second, I was really going to keep the coke, tell Gene I sold it and then give him all the cash I had scrapped together. It wasn't anywhere near what he wanted. I was going to tell him they would pay me the rest in dribs and drabs.

"When I got back there, around twenty minutes after he had kicked me out, he didn't answer when I knocked. I tried the door. It was open. You can figure out the rest. He was dead on the floor. I panicked and ran."

"Did anybody see you? Would anyone know that you were there?"

"I was smart enough to wipe my fingerprints off the door knob though I'm sure the police found them all over the apartment. That didn't worry me much. Marty and I went to his house one night recently. I could lie and say that's how my fingerprints were all over the place. But, I didn't find my purse."

"I thought you ran away?"

"I didn't run that quickly," a mighty Karen confessed. "I looked for the damn purse but I did it real quick. I remembered where I had put it. It wasn't there."

"So, where is it?"

Karen looked and Jeremy. There were no tears in either her eyes or her voice.

"I don't know. I do know that I think I'm in a lot of trouble and you have to help me."

*   *   *

It was late. People still milled around the streets. In the neon, eye-hurting lights of the stores that sold the fancy, flashy T-shirts and cheap, plastic jewelry, Jeremy and Sheraton could see the rebellious children working their way home.

Sitting in a small café that seemed filled with dust and shadows of old ghosts, Pris had joined the two men for some cappuccino, a few pastries (if Sheraton would permit himself to turn his eye's the other way) and some serious talk.

Pris listened to an eager Sheraton first and then sat patiently while the story was dragged out of Jeremy. She idly dipped her finger into the whipped cream but lost track of time as the puzzling afternoon was replayed for her benefit.

"That's some crazy marriage those two have going for them," she said when Jeremy had finished. "She doesn't know what he's up to and vice-versa."

Sheraton nibbled at a piece of Jeremy's chocolate frosted pastry. "Funny how both of them seemed to end up with Gene, each in his or her own way."

"I see nothing funny about it," Jeremy complained, finding nothing soothing in the pastry before him. "They both knew what Gene was and what he was involved with. Why would two normal people go to such lengths to get themselves entangled with such a trouble maker?"

Somewhere within the pink painted, cavern-like room, an espresso machine let out a whooshing hiss as it frothed milk. Bright, recently polished brass gleamed as if it were taking the darkness of the night and subtracting it into brightness.

"If you feel that way," Pris said, "why stop with Karen and Marty? Why not include Barbara and Jazz as well? It seems that, except for you two, everybody was beating a track to Gene's front door."

"Especially on the night that he died," Jeremy commented. He was in no mood for anything. His afternoon excursion with Karen set him into a bleak frame of mind. Ideally, he would have wanted to stop all the talk but, try as he might, he was powerless to do so. A certain amount of interest, which was coupled with curiosity, made it an impossible topic for even him to avoid.

"Before we go checking to see where our own mothers were that night," Pris said, "let's stop and look at some other interesting angles.

"Do you realize that Gene seems to have threatened to blackmail everybody?"

"Still, they kept going back for more," Jeremy said. "Why would they allow him to bamboozle them like that? That's what I don't understand."

"Pity," Sheraton said, sipping a long gulp of his coffee. "Gene was a pathetic figure to them. Subconsciously, of course."

"He was trying to drive them into the poor house when he wasn't busy turning them into drug pushers and you think that makes him an object to be pitied?"

"A man can say or threaten you with anything. It doesn't mean that he is going to do what he swears he will do." Sheraton seemed to have retained most of his fighting spirit. Instead of losing it, as Jeremy had hoped and wished, it was intensifying if anything.

"Gene was many things," Sheraton explained. "I don't think that, intentionally, he was a blackmailer at heart. If he was, people wouldn't have liked him at all."

"That's true," Pris said. "I don't ever send a Valentine's Day card to the people who have tried to blackmail me."

Sheraton giggled but persisted in presenting his point. "I think that Gene probably used more drugs than he sold. Everything we've heard about him-especially the blackmailing part-shows a rather weak man. It would have been rather easy for him to become an addict."

"So he was bluffing Karen, Marty and who knows who else to feed his habit?" Jeremy sounded bitter and very angry. "That makes him sick, not a candidate to get sympathy."

"All this psychological mumbo-jumbo about Gene is well and fine," Pris said. "However, it doesn't start to explain who killed the man. Remember, the list of people who went to his house that night is growing by leaps and bounds.

"Maybe he was a man who needed both pity and help. I'll grant you that, instead of giving him money, they should have sat and had a long chat with him and tried to help him through his problems. They didn't do that. One reason might have been because either Karen or Marty honestly believed that Gene would blackmail them."

"Good Lord," Sheraton gasped. "Then you think that one of them killed him?"

"I don't know, Sheraton. I'm just telling you how I can see it when I look at the picture one way. Tilting my head, I can see that if they were so ready to give into his demands, then maybe they were too weak to kill anybody.

"The point I'm trying to make is, we have people like the Sanders and then Jazz. They all risked their lives to make Gene happy. Yes. I know. That's something that bears looking into but, not now. Later we'll ponder the mysteries of the universe and why they were willing to make fools out of themselves. Right now, I wonder how far he really managed to push them."

"Pris is right," Jeremy agreed. "We know only what Karen, Marty and Jazz told us. That, naturally, was only as much of the story as they thought we should know. Their total dedication to Gene and subliminal desire to be a Bride of Christ-with Gene playing the title role in that piece-is a problem that they have to handle by themselves.

"When we present ourselves to others, the most natural thing to do is to try and come across as sweet, innocent and kind."

"You and I should try that route sometime, eh Jeremy?" Pris teased.

"It happens to be true though. The old cliché about 'There are two sides to every story' happens to be true most of the time. When we relate a personal incident, we always have a tendency to cast ourselves as the hero of the piece or the one who was spat upon up to the point where we had to defend ourselves.

"Marty and Karen were probably a lot more honest than Jazz was in speaking to us. I don't think Jazz played the part of the drug pusher who didn't get any love from his source and enjoyed the part. Gene, perhaps in his stoned state, went too far and pushed people about unmercifully. You can push even the most sanguine and docile person only so far before they'll push back. Hold in the resentment long enough and become frustrated for an extended period and who knows how crazy you can become when you finally let go."

"Speaking of letting go," Pris said after Jeremy finished. "Just because Barbara doesn't hold anything back, don't think it lets her off the hook. If Gene withheld his love and affection toward the others, why should he shower it upon the likes of her?"

"Good point," Sheraton said. "If only Barbara weren't so crazy to begin with. I mean, you can't believe anything she says. In her mind, she has trouble differentiating between fact and her own recently created fiction. Barbara might seriously believe her own story about the love affair she and Gene shared even if they did nothing more intimate than spit at each other from across a room once."

"It would be easy to pin the rap on her and then just try to go with your lives," Pris said, wishing for another cup of coffee. She appeased herself by studying the selection of flaky pastries instead while she tried to decide which would do the least damage to her already sagging body. "The only thing is, if the police ever find out half of what you men know, it won't be that easy. Jazz, Karen and Marty can get into a lot of trouble if, for no other reason, not reporting Gene's death to the proper authorities."

"They were scared and confused," Sheraton said, lamely trying to get himself to believe it.

"When Karen and Marty got to our place that night, neither of them seemed the least bit agitated," Jeremy reminded him. "They had just both seen a dead body-probably, I hope, their first. Yet, neither one was exceptionally upset over it."

"Jazz was a wreck," Pris said. "But, Jeremy's right. Karen and Marty were cool. Very cool. They handled it well."

"It could have been shock," Sheraton told her. "It effects some people like that."

"It could have been," Pris said, finishing her cappuccino. "Or, it could have been a careful performance. One, or even both of them, might be quite the actor."

*   *   *

Pris enjoyed the coffee and the company but, as they got closer to their stomping ground, she begged off from their offer to see her home.

"Thanks," she said, sounding slightly nervous and a wee bit giddy. "I think I'll hang out for a little while longer."

Behind her, discreetly tucked between a bank and an off-Broadway theater, was a woman's bar. Done up like a bit of whimsical gingerbread, Jeremy had once explained the rules of the house to Sheraton. No men in the gay women's bar just as some rougher, more serious-minded men's bars disapproved of female patrons. It was a sore spot between many liberal minded gay men and women. Mixing at a disco was all well and good. But, when the bar was determined to give itself the persona of being an earnest cruise bar, it was only one sex at a time if you please.

"She feels the same way about that silly, unwritten law as we do," Sheraton said. In his heart, much like Jeremy, he had found a warmth of feelings cropping up toward the woman. He already considered her a friend. So did Jeremy which was the highest accolade as he didn't mingle or become friendly with others easily.

Although it was a Sunday night-the traditional point where parties ended earlier than Saturday because the work week loomed ahead-there were still a smattering of crowds grouped into circles all around Sheridan Square. People who tried to wring every minute out of having fun and avoiding more weighty topics like work.

"Amazing," Jeremy said as he checked his watch. "Don't these people ever need any sleep or, am I the only one who goes to bed tired and wakes up more so?"

"Jeremy." Sheraton's hand touched his arm as he froze in his tracks. "Isn't that Jazz over there?"

Jeremy turned but could only see the queue of restless people standing in front of the automatic bank teller machines.

"Going into the Duchess," Sheraton said.

"The women there couldn't be that drunk and I don't think anyone could be that dumb," Jeremy said, still standing in the same spot. "They'll know it's a guy dressed in drag and bounce him."

"I'm certain it was Jazz," Sheraton insisted, crossing over to the triangle patch of cement that divided Seventh Avenue South. "Jeremy, do you know who was with him? It was Alan."

"Gene's brother?" Jeremy found himself immediately involved in the area where he was so determined to stay clear away from. "Was Alan in drag too?"

Before Sheraton could reply, a short and squat woman appeared at the door of the bar. She was wearing a lavender sweat shirt, the sleeves rolled up past the elbow, and was blocking the entrance to the bar. In front of her, looking as if he were pleading to get inside, was Jazz.

Sheraton and Jeremy stepped closer to the entrance and heard the woman's determined, no-nonsense voice as she tried to get rid of Jazz.

"There are plenty more places," she said gruffly. "Just keep walking."

"Just for a minute," Jazz answered in a highly strung falsetto of a voice that wouldn't fool anyone. "I have to use the ladies' room."

"So do the ladies that are already here. Move it."

"Do you know what the bathrooms are like in those other places?" Jazz's voice was getting high pitched. "It'll only be for a minute. Please. I'll pay the cover charge, powder my nose and be right out again."

Unsympathetically, the woman shot both arms out and across the doorway as if her limbs were dead bolts.

"Rules," she said sternly. "Now, get out of here both of you. Hey!" There was a surprised pause in her voice. She put her arms down and turned wildly around in a full circle. "That other one, the guy who was with you, where the hell is he?"

"Yes Jazz," Sheraton said, coming out of the shadows and linking his arm through his friends. "Where is Alan?"

"Alan?" Jazz was confused and let out a squeal of laughter. "Why, I'm unescorted tonight. At least I was until I met you."

"Save the southern belle performance for when you audition for *A Streetcar Named Desire*," Jeremy said to Jazz.

"I just had to use the rest facilities," Jazz stuttered. "This sweet lady was about to let me enter."

"Like hell I was!"

"You can use the bathroom in our place," Jeremy said.

Jazz began to shake slightly. "Why, that's so sweet of you but, honestly, I couldn't impose."

"Do you three men have to stand here?" The bouncer asked sternly. "It's bad for business."

Jeremy stared her down. "Yeah. It might make the place seem as if it were fun and fair."

"You don't see me putting on leather chaps and trying to crash into some of those cowboy bars up the block," she challenged.

"It's not a topic I want to get into right now," Jeremy said, turning to Jazz.

"Before you go anywhere," the bouncer said to Jazz. "Where the hell did your friend run off to anyway? If he's inside—"

"I told you, I came here alone." Jazz held his cupid's bow mouth in a tight line of contempt.

Jeremy took hold of Jazz's other arm and he and Sheraton escorted him to the street.

"What's going on here, Jazz?" Jeremy didn't bother with preambles. He immediately launched into what promised to be a full attack.

Taking a softer approach, Sheraton asked: "What were you doing downtown with Alan?"

"We met on the subway."

"You rode the subway dressed up like that?" Jeremy asked, taking into account Jazz's short skirt and sequined blouse.

With a toss of his head that caused a hundred strands of synthetic hair to go casting off into the night wind, Jazz answered: "Everybody thought I was just a big, beautiful doll."

"Listen Barbie, tell us where Ken ran off to just now."

It was a direct order and Jeremy delivered it with such force and strength that even Sheraton found himself unable to stop him.

"We met and exchanged a hello," Jazz said. "He and I met once or twice but he certainly wasn't my beau."

"Do you realize how serious everything is right now," Sheraton said as he managed to angle Jazz into a recessed nook between the bar and the bank. "All sorts of crazy things and odd questions are being asked. One of them will certainly be about your friendship with Alan.

"Tell me something honestly, is Alan taking up the slack of selling drugs?"

"No," Jazz said primly. "And I'm not carrying any. You can strip me and search me if you want."

"That might be the best offer I've had all day but I'm not interested," Jeremy answered. "Instead of putting your hands on the wall and standing spread eagle, why not come clean and tell us what you're up to tonight?"

"You know I like to go out nights when I get dressed up," Jazz said softly. "I fail to see what all the fuss is about."

"Too many things have been happening recently. None of them make any sense."

Jazz lowered his eyes. "You think that I had something to do with Gene's death, don't you?"

"We think you're not telling us everything you know," Sheraton said kindly. "One of the things that you might be holding back is, if Gene didn't get along with his family, how come he had Alan over to his place?"

"And," Jeremy continued, "how did you and Alan become such close buddies that you travel around town together?"

"I could be very friendly."

"Cut the act," Jeremy shouted. People turned but, on Sheridan Square, it took a lot more than a man yelling at a drag queen to cause them to become interested. "It's not working. You can put on the seductress act all you like. We're not buying it."

"Alan wanted to talk to me," Jazz said. "I don't know about what. He just wanted to speak to me privately. I knew I would be down in the Village tonight and I asked him to meet me here. I picked the Duchess because, although it's gay, I thought he wouldn't be so nervous in a gay woman's bar. Besides, I was positive that no one that either of us knew would be there."

"You must know that the Duchess doesn't let men inside," Jeremy told him.

"They let me," Jazz insisted. "Not the cretin who was guarding the door tonight but, sometimes I can slip inside."

"And how were you going to explain Alan to the bouncer?"

"Once I got him inside, they wouldn't have raised a fuss if he left the patrons alone."

"What did Alan want to talk to you about?" Sheraton asked.

"I don't know," Jazz said. "You and that barbarian at the gate scared him away."

"That's another thing," Sheraton said to Jeremy after Jazz mumbled some excuse and ran off, high heels clacking on the pavement, into the night. "Where the heck did Alan go off to so quickly? And, how come we didn't see him leave?"

"It's only natural Sheraton. When a guy is looking at a drag queen, nothing else around him seems to register."

"I guess we were both staring at Jazz," Sheraton admitted reluctantly. "Still, it does seem a bit odd."

That were walking up the steps to their apartment. They paused at Pris' door and knocked on the off chance that she might have gotten home by then. There was no answer so they continued up another flight of steps.

"The hall light is out," Jeremy complained. "Damn it to hell and back. It's hard enough trying to find the keyhole with the lights on."

Sheraton surprised Jeremy by producing a small box of matches from his pocket.

"I got them from the café," he giggled. "I know how we're always hunting around looking for a match from time to time and I thought that it would be a good idea to start collecting some for when the pilot light on the kitchen range goes out."

Just then, footsteps sounded from the landing above.

Jeremy asked Sheraton to hold the match closer to the keyhole and neither man paid much attention to the sound of some neighbor leaving their apartment.

It wasn't until Sheraton looked up that he saw a sight that caused him to become frightened.

Two figures in baggy, black shirts and pants were sneaking down the steps. Over their heads were pulled down black, knitted ski caps. One had an embroidered figure of Mickey Mouse on it; the other Snoopy.

"Jeremy." Was all that Sheraton was able to get out of his mouth before the two hooded figures lurched down on top of them.

Sheraton felt the cold, marble floor of the hallway as he was pushed down and shoved into a corner.

Around his throat, Jeremy felt the long nails and the pressure of fingers tightening. He began to struggle but the attack had been so quick and he had been taken by such surprise that he was still reeling from the shock.

Slowly, painfully, the fingers around his throat tightened. Jeremy could feel himself sliding down onto the floor. His head banged against his own door and, immediately after the blow to the back of his head, he felt a drifting, woozy sort of pillowing effect as if he were sinking into deep, warm clouds.

Then, everything went black.

SEVEN

Slowly, as if in a jerky series of slow-motion, flickering pictures running past his eyes, Jeremy found himself coming to again.

An ache, deadly dull and throbbing unmercifully, seemed to be shooting in lighting bolt flashes across the inside of his head.

"Be quiet," a voice said, stiff and refined. There was a certain amount of authority there and something else. Jeremy felt it was impatience.

Slowly, willing himself to do so with a force that really wasn't working now, Jeremy opened his eyes. He was staring at a white painted ceiling. Firecracker red paint had been recently applied to the moldings and, even through the painful cobweb's that seemed to be frosted over his eyes, it looked wet. Wet and strangely familiar somehow.

"Sheraton." Jeremy's lips were dry and felt cracked. He tried to sit up, indeed he thought he had been sitting up. He had to close his eyes and mechanically willed his body into the somewhat unfamiliar process. His head was so racked with sharp pain that it wasn't until he opened his eyes again that he realized he was still lying flat on his back.

"He's right here too," the voice said.

Enough of his previous life came flooding back. In between the beating drums of pain that were pounding fiercely between his ears and behind his eyes, Jeremy could remember Gene's death and the confusions and suspicions that arose from his death. He also remembered something else. Childhood cartoons and flashes of Walt Disney reading the Sunday funny papers.

He opened his eyes and tried a childhood trick of his. To himself, Jeremy mentally said: "Pain, be gone."

The ceiling, slightly shaking, bobbed into view. He resisted the urge to squeeze his eyes shut again and tried to hold onto the image until he could figure out where he was.

Pris' face-puffy eyes and pale cheeks-loomed largely in front of him now. It was the sweetest, and funniest, face he could ever remember seeing.

"Is that you Pris or am I seeing another mask?"

"I never claimed to be a raving beauty," she said in a soft voice. "Still, I don't look half as bad as all that! You make it sound like I'm all set to play Freddy Kruger's mother."

"Sheraton. Is Sheraton here?"

"Sleeping soundly on the other sofa," she said, applying a cold, damp cloth to his forehead. Water dripped into his eyes.

"What happened?"

"That's suppose to be my question. I came back from the Duchess-alone if that makes any difference to you-and I found the two of you lying in the hallway."

"How did we get here?" Jeremy struggled himself up. By putting some of his weight on his elbows, he managed to half lift the upper portion of his body to a right angle with the bed of the sofa he was on. "By the way, where is here?"

"I've been meaning to ask you to see my humble abode," Pris said, wringing the cloth in a small, Pyrex bowl of clean water. "I thought your first trip would be at a more festive time."

"Tell me something, were you and Sheraton mugged before or after you got stinking drunk?"

"Drunk?" Jeremy had seen Sheraton's form lying across the room. He looked passively sedate and unharmed. "What gave you the idea that we were pissed?"

"When I carried you here-"

"*You carried us?*"

"Try not to be offensive," Pris warned him, applying a fresh cloth to his head. "Besides from insulting women all over the world, you'll also get one dyke very, very angry with you."

"Sorry," Jeremy said, falling back down on the sofa. Lying prone, he asked: "After you carried us up here, what did you do then? Chop a couple of cords of wood for the fire so we wouldn't freeze to death or did you go out and hunt for some food?"

"Neither. I debated whether I should call for a doctor. I decided that you must have been drunk and just fell down in the hall. The light on your floor burnt out."

"As hard living as I might seem to you, I don't get tanked every time a light bulb burns out somewhere in Gotham."

"When I asked you what happened, you said something about being attacked by Snoopy. Now, tell me that you didn't have a few too many."

"I was not mugged by Snoopy," Jeremy said. "Sheraton was. I was attacked by Mickey Mouse."

"Oh. If you had said that the first time I asked you, I wouldn't have thought anything odd about it. Only last week I saw Fred Flintstone rolling a drunk."

"Snoopy and Mickey Mouse came down the stairs and hit us," Jeremy said, too weak to realize how this actually sounded.

"Of course. Now, if you'll forgive me, I'll go next door and ask Blondie and Dagwood if they have any more ice for your compress."

"Pris, you have to believe me. Sheraton and I were mugged."

"I'm not being flippant. I do believe you, Jeremy. God knows that I don't want to but if you say Lassie—"

"Snoopy."

"If you say you were attacked by a cartoon character, I believe it."

Jeremy was dizzy and had a bout of nausea attacking him. Through it all, he was still able to hear that Pris did believe him. But, if she did, why the smart ass remarks?

"Sheraton has a bump on his head. You have a bump and some nasty marks around your throat. I didn't notice them until I slid down the top of your turtleneck sweater. That was when I knew that I should have called a doctor."

"Why didn't you?"

Pris seemed to find the bowl of water very interesting just about the time that Jeremy asked his question.

"Pris, what happened? Is it Sheraton?"

"Sheraton's going to be fine. He came to first. He's sleeping now. True, he didn't say anything about Disney on parade. He must need glasses. I could have sworn he muttered something about Rocky and Bullwinkle."

"You mean we were attacked by four instead of only two?"

"I was making a joke," Pris sighed. "Jeremy. Both you and Sheraton are going to be OK."

"You've got a strange tone in your voice now. What is it?"

"We'll talk about it in the morning. You can stay here tonight. I suppose that both my maidenhood and my reputation will withstand one night with two men sacked out in my living room."

"Pris. What are you holding back?"

"I was at the Duchess after I left you," she said, reaching for his hand and holding it tightly. "I heard a commotion outside and, snoop that I am, I went to investigate.

"That man you told me about-Detective Lawrence-was arresting your friend."

"Friend?"

"Jazz."

This time, Jeremy was able to conquer the pain enough so that he shot straight up like a bolt.

"What?"

"Lie down," Pris ordered him, gently applying pressure to his shoulder with her free hand.

"Detective Lawrence arrested Jazz? For what? Is it really a crime to impersonate a lady?"

"I did it for years and I never got busted for it."

"Pris, do you know why they arrested Jazz?"

"I couldn't find out from Detective Lawrence. I rushed to the pay phone and tried to call up you and Sheraton. When I didn't get an answer, I managed to catch Detective Stone. He was just as nasty as his partner but he told me that they were arresting Jazz and planning on charging him with Gene's death."

"But Jazz didn't kill Gene."

"How do you know that, Jeremy?"

"Sheraton told me so."

Pris began to rub his hand with hard, swift circles.

"I don't think that will hold up in a court of law." She turned her head and looked at Sheraton's sleeping form across the room. "But, then again, it just might. If I know anything about Sheraton, he just might prove that Jazz is innocent."

*   *   *

"There's a security here," Sheraton said, slowly sipping a fruit juice and trying to sound in a lot better shape than he felt.

"Yeah," Jeremy responded, trying to puff up a pillow that didn't sag in any of the same spots as he did. "She's a great friend. We also wouldn't have to be dependent upon her hospitality if we could steer clear of this whole mess."

"But, how can we?" Sheraton put down the small glass and rested his head against Jeremy's shoulder. "Jeremy, the people concerned in this aren't strangers-they're all our friends."

"Sheraton, darling, has it ever occurred to you that our friends are strangers to us?" Jeremy was gruff and the aches and pains that he was suffering through made him especially cranky. "We *thought* we knew these people. Do we honestly? Can you sit there and tell me that you suspected that somebody like Karen would chase after a man and even contemplate having an affair? How about Marty? He's sweet and sometimes being too sweet can be a vice. I still have trouble accepting the fact that Marty forked over all that money to Gene just because Gene caught him having a mixed drink in a gay bar."

"You think that Marty might have been up to something other than a harmless drink during happy hour?"

"He certainly sounds as if he were trying to tell you something along those lines."

"Look, I can well imagine how tough Karen can be. I'm sure that she wouldn't ever let Marty live it down if he had been caught in a gay bar-or even a straight one for that matter. But, if Marty was doing nothing more than having a drink with some friends, how far could she go with her complaining? Stopping to have a few quick one's before a guy goes home to the little woman isn't exactly unheard of; nor is it a crime of treason. However, if Karen were to have some proof from Gene where Marty had been caught with his pants down—"

"I doubt that," Sheraton said. "Neither do you."

"OK. Marty isn't interested in sex. I guess if he were, he wouldn't have married Karen. How about Gene? You're risking life and limb-especially mine-to avenge his death.

"So far, we've found out that Gene was a drug addict, a dope pusher, a would-be home wrecker and a possible blackmailer. I'm sorry the man is dead but, let's face it. He's hardly a prime example of humanitarianism."

"I agree. He should have been punished for the things that he tried to do." Sheraton snuggled closer to Jeremy. "He didn't deserve to die for them though.

"Now. How about Jazz? You can't possibly think that he actually murdered Gene?"

"I don't. I also don't like the idea of a cross-dresser being locked up in a city jail any more than you do. I'm not dumb. I can imagine what life must be like for a guy thrown into the Tombs wearing panty hose. I think that Jazz should get good legal counsel. They'll advice him as to his rights and they'll also examine any evidence that Detective Lawrence may have against him."

"Why Jazz? That's what makes me angry."

"Maybe you'd be happier if Detective Lawrence had arrested me?"

"Of course not," Sheraton said. "It's just that Jazz is too innocent and too kind. He's not prepared for something like this. You saw how fragile he was the night of Gene's death."

"I also saw him trying to lie through his teeth when we saw him and Alan together last night. I'm not saying he killed anything except maybe fashion: he just isn't being totally honest."

"He was in love with Gene. You suspected that as well as I did."

"I can't believe that anybody would even want to like a man like Gene," Jeremy complained, pulling the duvet Pris had given them up around their collected chins. "It could only be an example of opposites attracting."

"Why is it," Sheraton asked, "that I keep coming back to Barbara? Do you think she's involved in this? It would be just like a womanizing egotist like Detective Lawrence to take the word of somebody like Barbara."

"And why would Barbara want to hurt Jazz?"

"Because she's guilty?"

Jeremy stiffened a little and began to massage his neck. "If that's the case, then Jazz won't need us. He's innocent and he'll be released."

"Barbara isn't a good actress to any of us because we know her," Sheraton reminded him. "We expect her to say and do crazy things. We don't seriously consider anything she may say. The police don't know her as well as we do. If she went there, sobbing and teary eyed and told them about how close Gene was to her, they may feel sorry for her."

"The lady needs all the pity she can get."

"Not at Jazz's expense," Sheraton insisted. "It's Barbara. It has to be something that she told the police that got Jazz arrested."

Jeremy cupped Sheraton's face in his hands. "Honey, I promised to always love you, never cheat on you and to try not to complain too much when you put celery in macaroni salad. I've been pretty good about that. I never told you that I would play a detective for you. Truthfully, I don't know how. Neither do you."

"We can't let Jazz go through this alone. We're going to help him."

"How?"

"Well, Pris knows this attorney-"

"Sheraton, how do you know?"

"When you were brushing your teeth, Pris and I discussed it and she said—"

"What is this? One day I'm a happy man with a cute, blonde lover. Today I'm Ricky Ricardo who's got Lucy and Ethel plotting and scheming behind his back."

Softly, with a gentle determinableness that couldn't be avoided, Sheraton said: "We have to help Jazz and we are."

"Right," Jeremy said, slipping down on Pris' sofa bed and staring blankly into the night. "Here we go. I can't wait to see which cartoon character mugs, robs or maims us next time."

* * *

"I'm not too sure about this," Jeremy complained as he slipped into a fresh shirt.

"Relax," Sheraton answered. "Pris said this woman is very good."

"I don't know about any of this. How much trust can you put into an attorney that Pris met in a bar?"

Jeremy's fears and Sheraton's concerns were about a woman whose services Pris offered to them. She wasn't exactly a friend but Pris felt that she was honest and reliable which prompted Jeremy to ask, "Are you sure then that she's a lawyer?"

The woman, straight back and long, salt and pepper colored hair flung down in a casual style, seemed serious and earnest.

"I've gotten some preliminaries," she said, adjusting a pair of wire rimmed spectacles. There was a brisk, almost unpolished way about her that seemed to preclude any formalities over and beyond a curt handshake. Studying the papers, the lawyer seemed to keep her features in total check. It was hard to judge what she was thinking or how concerned she was about Jazz's outcome in the matter.

"There seems some evidence that the police latched onto," she finally said. The former papers went into a stainless steel brief case and were replaced by new forms. "Under the victims fingernails were traces of skin. The police labs reported that this skin exhibited both male hair and an over-abundance of cosmetics. Base make-up and so forth."

"And that makes the police believe that Jazz killed Gene?" Sheraton had peeked over Jeremy's shoulder enough to have become familiar with certain passages in his lovers murder mysteries. There were always clues-hairs and tell-tale signs. Those, printed up on cheap stock-always seemed so conclusive.

"There were certain signs in the deceased's apartment that indicated that a struggle had taken place," the woman said, adjusting her glasses but not looking up at them. "A small wooden cabinet containing dry goods such as corn flakes was overturned in a struggle."

"Then Gene did put up a fight," Jeremy said. It made him feel better to believe that, in the last round, Gene had at least tried to defend himself.

"A struggle," the woman rectified. "The particles that were found under his nails show signs that the man tried to ward off his attacker."

"That doesn't make sense," Sheraton pointed out. "Gene was shot. You don't defend yourself from a gun by trying to scratch your killer's face with your hands."

"I really wouldn't know," she said. The glasses came off and a small smile played upon her face. "I think what the both of you are trying to do for your friend, Jazz, is commendable."

"The lab reports," an embarrassed Jeremy said. "Did they tell you whose hair it could be that was found under Gene's nails?"

"Preliminary reports say that the skin type matches up with a fair skinned male in his mid thirties."

Jazz, both knew, fit that rather skimpy description.

"What happens now?" Pris asked, hearing the lull in the conversation and trying to expedite matters.

"Bail will be set for Jazz," her friend responded. "It will be rather high."

"Because Jazz was booked on a possible murder charge?"

The lawyer rubbed her fingers together and then over and across some documents lying on her lap.

"It seems that, when he was arrested, Jazz was in possession of drugs."

"That's impossible," Sheraton exclaimed.

"The police provided me with a listing of what was in the man's pocketbook," the woman said, managing to mix the words 'man' and 'pocketbook' into her sentence without any signs of discomposure. "True, it was only a trace of cocaine but, to make the state's case against your friend more solid, they will use that against the suspect."

Jeremy asked, "What has Jazz said about the charges?"

"I'm afraid that your friend hasn't said anything to deny his guilt in the affair. In fact, he's said nothing at all. True, he did go into hysterics but he didn't deny the charges."

"Nor did he confirm them," Sheraton said sternly.

The woman seemed to have softened in appearance somehow. She looked smaller and more human.

"Let me ask you a personal question. Just how well do you really know Jazz?"

Without thinking, Sheraton said: "Well enough to know that he's innocent."

"You didn't hesitate," she smiled. "You understand that he's in a particularly difficult situation. The police still have many prejudices against gays-as do a majority of people in other professions. A gay man who dresses in leather or a business suit may get away from these prejudices a little. Once it's reported that a man was arrested in a dress, it's bound to work against the accused in court. One thing that even an innocent man accused of a crime needs is sympathy. Many in our society consider transvestites as pathetic and strange."

"So then, you're telling us that Jazz has all the odds against him before he even stands trial," Jeremy said.

"I believe that he deserves a fair trial," the woman said. "I, how-ever, am not the court, judge or jury."

Pris shook her head. "Why won't Jazz scream and yell and tell the world that he's innocent?"

"Because," her friend replied, "he may be scared."

"Thank you," Sheraton said. "Where do we go from here?"

"We wait for them to set bail and work with Jazz from there," she said, folding up the papers and tucking them back into her brief case. "It's scary for him and for you I dare say."

"Scary?" Sheraton said, avoiding eye contact with Jeremy. "It's not scary. It's a challenge. You think that he's innocent: I know that Jazz is innocent."

"Then Lord help us all," the woman said grimly.

*   *   *

Jeremy knew that, given Sheraton's seemingly bottomless amount of patience and perseverance, he could usually get his way in a great variety of circumstances. Knowing this, it shouldn't have surprised him when he followed his lover into the West Tenth Street Police station house.

Seeing Detective Lawrence standing in a corner of the room, coffee cup in one hand while the other hand was wildly waving about in circular gestures to make a point, Jeremy felt himself wanting to retract to the exit.

"You do believe in facing the lion right in his den," Jeremy said, the fluorescent lighting shining a bit too bright and the blue uniformed men and women milling about putting too much fear into him.

"Oh my God," Detective Lawrence said, turning automatically and calling his partner to come join in on the fun. "Don't tell me that you pussycats are going to confess and help me get three fag's off the streets?"

"We're here because of Jazz," Sheraton said.

"Jazz?" Detective Lawrence looked at Detective Stone and seemed to enjoy himself immensely. "Can you describe this Jazz person you're looking for, pussycat?"

Jeremy wasn't about to be jerked about by any feline loving officer of the law.

"Tall, blonde and arrested by you last night."

"I arrest many bad guys. Could you be a little more explicit?"

"Why are we playing this silly game?" Sheraton asked, refusing to stoop to the man's level no matter how much he was generally willing to compromise. "That man is innocent. He didn't kill Gene."

"Then who did?"

"Maybe," Detective Stone interrupted, "this is a confession. Should I go and get somebody to take down the confession?"

"Why don't you go and get yourself some coffee and leave us alone for a minute," Jeremy said to him.

"You're mighty sure of yourself," Detective Stone said. "Sort of cocky, aren't you?"

"You've been waiting a long time to use that word, haven't you?"

"I've been waiting an even longer time to bash a few heads," Detective Stone announced; a wild, dementedly maniac smile bouncing across his face.

"Can we see Jazz?" Sheraton asked the men.

"Why? Do you want to slip him a file inside a tube of lipstick?"

"Maybe they think we allow murder suspects to have intercourse during visiting hours?" Detective Lawrence laughed.

"Maybe we think you've got the wrong person behind bars," Jeremy exploded.

"Oh yeah, pussycat? Then, who did kill your friend?"

"We don't know," Sheraton said. "Yet."

"Well, why the hell didn't you say so." Detective Lawrence stood next to his partner and tried to bond himself with the man to form some sort of powerful, frightening team. "I'm sure if the Commissioner knew that you were working on the case, he wouldn't have bothered the rest of the force. Now, you two pussycats sit right here while I go and arrange for a limo to pick your friend up. Maybe, if the chauffeur doesn't get tied up in cross town traffic, we can have Jazz home in time to watch Ophra."

"Do you think that Jazz killed Gene?" Sheraton asked, disgusted by the flip, petty attitude but refusing to show that he was nearing his boiling point now. "You have evidence—"

"We have proof," Detective Stone stated.

"You don't have a confession from Jazz," Jeremy said. "That's important too, isn't it?"

"He'll confess," a confident Detective Stone replied.

"Sure he will," Jeremy answered. "A few more hours in that hell hole and he'll admit to being a gun runner during the war of 1812."

Detective Lawrence grabbed a small, tubular steel chair and hoisted it around so that he could prop his foot up on it.

"Why is everybody so interested in this Jazz character?"

Sheraton didn't know Detective Lawrence well enough (and hoped he never would) to understand if the man was making a blind statement or telling a fact. Trying not to fall too easily into any planned traps, he asked: "Who else is interested in Jazz?"

"Besides that bull dozer of a lawyer that I understand you two pussycats hired, we've had a few other inquiries into his welfare. Imagine. Put a wig and falsies on a man and he's instantly innocent. Must be a new rider added to the constitution that the police department doesn't know about yet."

"Other people have asked you about Jazz?" Sheraton found this slightly confusing but very interesting. "Who?"

"Now pussycat, why should I tell you a blessed thing? I don't recall you or your boy friend treating either me or my partner very nicely when we dropped by your place."

Jeremy said, "Blame it on the caterer. They couldn't deliver the cheese rolls and canapes in time. We did have somebody ready to start the colored lights but you left before we could give him the high sign."

"You don't have a damn bit of evidence to prove that your sick friend is innocent, do you?"

"We have as much evidence that Jazz is innocent as you do that he's guilty," Jeremy said.

"Everybody sure is anxious about this Jazz pussycat," Detective Lawrence said, sounding as if he were again trying to lure them somewhere.

"OK," Sheraton said, biting his lower lip and praying for patience. "Who is everybody?"

"Some mysterious phone calls," Detective Stone said. "And the brother of the guy who was killed made a personal appearance here, just like you."

"Alan came here?" It shouldn't have surprised him, but Sheraton found that a bit more than just odd. After last night, it seemed that Alan was tied into his brothers death but he couldn't quite see how.

"Maybe," Jeremy said, "you can understand then why Sheraton and I are here. Everybody who knows Jazz can see that he's not a killer."

"Pussycat, you're assuming. I didn't say that the others gave a flying fuck if we were warming up the electric chair for Jazz. They just wanted to make sure that he was safely tucked away in a nice safe place."

"Prison cell," Jeremy responded. "Why do you make it sound like you've got Jazz stashed away somewhere in a *Motel 6* room near an interstate?"

"You think that drag queen is innocent? Well, nobody else seemed to care about anything. They just wanted to make sure he was locked up and out of harm's way."

"The people on the phone," Sheraton asked. "Did they give you their names?"

"Sure," Detective Stone laughed. "Along with their home address and blood type."

"An anonymous phone call or two and you're using that as proof of Jazz's guilt?"

"We're using the fact that your friends facial hair was discovered under the nails of the victim," Detective Stone shouted. His face was a puffy shadow of enraged purple. "We don't care about phone calls or cryptic notes. We regard them much in the same way as we think about you and your boy friend here-the work of a coward and a nut case."

"Did Jazz have any idea how his facial hair got under Gene's finger-nails?" Sheraton asked, feeling that this was going to be a pivotal point that might eventually incriminate Jazz-probably sooner than later.

"No," Detective Lawrence said. "He just looked shocked. Probably shocked that it was his facial hair we found and not his pubic hair."

"Could we see him?" Jeremy asked, using a fearless bravado. "We want to see Jazz."

Detective Stone was listening with a smirk on his face. He had quieted down. An officer rushed over to him and handed him a piece of paper. He read it, reread it again and then slipped it to his partner.

"It looks," Detective Lawrence said, after reading the note, "that your friend has been a busy, little boy."

"What happened?" Sheraton asked, his heart sinking rapidly as his imagination went wild.

"You can't see Jazz," Detective Lawrence said, still smiling. "At least, you can't see him in jail. Try the hospital."

"Hospital?"

Detective Lawrence kicked the chair he had been using as a foot rest and sent it crashing against a wall.

"Hospital, pussycat. Your friend tried to kill himself."

EIGHT

Pris' attorney friend looked hopeful but sounded doubtful.

"You have to understand," she said, looking briefly around her small, cluttered office as if it were a bad dream she was trying to escape. "The police still have a few problems with certain types of prisoners."

"How did Jazz get a weapon to try to slash his wrists?" Jeremy asked, realizing how harsh and curt he sounded but beyond caring for the gift wrapping aspect of words and their delivery now.

"It was a hair clip," the woman said, shoving her glasses up her nose and trying to avoid looking at either man. "They took away his wig but, in Jazz's own hair, he had some sort of sharp edged clip that he used. I don't know why the metal detector he had to pass through didn't detect it-"

"Did they really bother with any of those formalities?" Jeremy asked before Sheraton could attempt to quiet him. "Or, did they see a cross dresser and become to busy having hysterical fits of laughter to do their jobs properly? Did they care if Jazz-in his distraught state-had a lethal weapon or not?"

The woman looked up. Her eyes were clear and almost as sharp as her voice. "I can understand why you're confused and concerned but—"

"But, the law is a lot different for drag queens than it is for others, isn't it?" Pris, feeling somewhat battered, was disgusted by what she was beginning to realize was a part of the justice system that wasn't generally talked about much.

"We're trying," her friend said, a concerned and optimistic note in his voice. "That's all I can tell you now. We're all trying."

*   *   *

Saint Vincent's hospital was an old, solid looking building that was within walking distance. Usually, it seemed to be undergoing constant renovations and construction. Expansions-costly, messy but understandable-were frequently under way.

Sheraton stopped for flowers. The cellophane wrapper, crackling in his hands every time he moved, held simple but colorful flowers. Jeremy didn't protest at either the thought or the cost of the gift though he secretly feared that they would never be allowed up to Jazz's room.

"I'm sorry," a crisp voiced nurse told them. "But, that patient isn't allowed visitors."

Was it his imagination, Jeremy wondered, or did she give them a particularly hostile stare? What was blipping on the computer terminal screen close to her face?

"Is there a supervisor we might speak to then?" Sheraton, undaunted as always, asked.

They were directed down a long, marble and stained glass hall. Inside the first room on the left, in a cubby hole that was cramped and dark but decorated with colorful cards and small curios, sat a small, gray haired woman.

She patiently listened to their story and even managed to smile once or twice but, when Sheraton had finished, she shook her head.

"I'm sorry," she kindly told them. "It's not the hospital rules that are keeping you from seeing your friend. The police department is in charge here and they aren't allowing him any visitors."

Jeremy exhaled a bodyful of exasperated air while Sheraton said, "But, we'd feel so much better if we could just give Jazz these flowers—"

"You'd feel better if you could see your friend for yourself," she said quite directly. "I don't blame you. Sometimes I think that it's the visitors who suffer more than our patients. You'd also like to speak to him and ask why he tried to take his life. It's only natural. However, I should tell you that it wouldn't help your friend now. Too many questions and all the confusion might only upset him even more.

"Now, I could see if I could smuggle your flowers into him but I'm afraid that's as far as I'm willing to go for anyone when it comes to bending the rules around here."

They thanked her and glumly walked down the antiseptic smelling corridor.

"It's not fair," Sheraton said in a breaking voice. "Jazz has been through so much recently."

"We all have."

Sheraton looked back and stared at the office they had just left.

"I bet that if she wanted to, she could have gotten us up there for a few minutes."

"And if she wanted to end up on the unemployment line, she could have had us up there while doing a jig down the corridor." Jeremy sighed again. He felt that it relieved a small part of the pressure building with him though, unknown to him, it only managed to discourage Sheraton every time he made the sound.

"How about Jazz's family?" Sheraton said quickly, his mind plotting and scheming. "I wonder if that rule applies to everybody or just us?"

"Now you're going and getting paranoid on me. That's not going to help much."

"I know but…" Sheraton stopped, tugged at Jeremy's sleeve and pulled him down a side corridor with a strength that Jeremy hadn't suspected that Sheraton had within him.

"Look," Jeremy hissed. "If this is some wild idea of yours, I'm not allowing it. We're not sneaking up to see Jazz."

"Jeremy," Sheraton whispered back. "Did you see who is at the reception desk now? It's Barbara."

"Great. Let's find the back door and get out of this place."

Through the echoing hallways, Barbara's voice carried. She was protesting long and loud over her denied request to visit Jazz.

"I'm sorry miss," the same nurse, staring at the same video terminal, said to Barbara. "It's against rules-"

"Do you know who I am?" Barbara's tone was daunting. "How dare you deny me permission to see that man! Why, he and I are practically man and wife."

"I couldn't care if you and he were Adam and Eve," the woman flatly informed Barbara. "It's against the rules."

"I don't follow rules; I make them. Now, get off your fat ass lady and get me the Surgeon General on the phone and make it snappy."

"He's out having a quick smoke," the woman answered. "Speaking of going out, you should do so now before I call security."

Sheraton and Jeremy poked their heads around the corner. They could see Barbara, decked out in an old fashioned Dior type suit complete with gold chains around her neck and multitudes of bubble sized beads comprising bracelets around both her arms.

"Maybe I got carried away," Barbara said, snapping open a patent leather pocketbook and pulling out a small handkerchief. "I'm sure that *you* want me to go up there."

"Only because it's on the same floor as our psycho ward."

Ignoring her, Barbara kept up her concerned act.

"Do you know what love is? True love?"

"She's a phony," Sheraton whispered excitedly. "Jeremy, she's going to tell that nurse that she and Jazz were lovers just like she insisted to the police that Gene was her lover."

Jeremy shrugged. "It must be nice to be so popular."

"I love him," Barbara sniffed, unfolding the handkerchief and wiping tears from her eyes. "He's like my little boy. I know he needs his mommy now."

"He needs his rest," the nurse replied tartly. "I also need to get back to my job. Now, if you're quite finished-"

Barbara threw down the dry handkerchief. "I am not a person who can be denied. Obviously you don't know how powerful and important I am!"

Picking up a phone, the nurse answered: "I'm sure you are, dear. Be sure to tell that to the guards who kick you out of here. I'm sure it will just brighten their day to no end."

Jeremy and Sheraton, without consulting the other but acting as if it were rehearsed, emerged from their hiding place and walked over to the front desk.

"Hello Barbara," Sheraton said.

"Oh?" Barbara seemed particularly unfazed.

"I think we have to have a talk."

*   *   *

A small, Tex-Mex themed restaurant on Bleecker Street was casual in it's presentation. In a world of hi-tech interior designs and ultra-modern decor bordering on the futuristic, it managed to survive with pale pink and green walls that looked sun faded, and white washed trim. There was an austerity about the place that directly focused one's attention onto the menu rather than the surroundings.

Jeremy and Sheraton escorted Barbara there for lunch. It was close to their apartment-too close, Jeremy worried at one point-but it had a laid-back, unpressured atmosphere that seemed as easy to slip into as the cat who sat in the large window sunning itself.

"Hardly a day goes by when I don't think of my beloved up in heaven," Barbara announced, crossing her arms across her heavily gold chained chest. "I can hardly think of anything else these days and my mind just doesn't absorb anything any longer. I pray to God for my man's soul. By the way, I never heard of half the fucking beer types this place has for sale. Most of them sound like Texas piss in a bottle."

Obviously, Barbara's prayers to God for her man's soul had been temporarily shelved by her born-again interest in Milwaukee.

"Everybody loved Gene," Sheraton said quietly.

"Yes," Barbara sighed, turning the menu over to the drink portion and studying the listing through squinting eyes. "He's gone and now I'm stuck in this slum."

Jeremy let his eyes cast out the window, beyond the sunning cat, and saw the tree lined street and quiet, ambient feeling that seemed to walk the street alongside the pedestrians.

"What is good to order in this place?" Barbara demanded. "I haven't been able to eat much recently. I'm sure both of you know how important it is for one to try and keep one's girlish figure."

Jeremy felt that his commiserating smile to Barbara was phony but he offset this against the fact that, so was Barbara.

Barbara ordered a drink and then jumped frantically up and went to the ladies room, nearly knocking over the table in her haste to get there.

Sheraton fairly jumped at Jeremy. "What are you up to inviting her here?"

"I thought you wanted to talk to her."

"Not at an expensive restaurant."

"Amazing," Jeremy laughed. "For years I avoided kissing the witch's face, not I'm kissing her ass for information.

"Look Sheraton, there's no sense in hoping that Barbara fell in the can so I have to make this fast.

"That list you're compiling-maybe it's not so far fetched as I thought it was. Now, today, with Jazz in such a serious position, I'm beginning to wonder if, maybe, you're not on the right track."

"I know we're on the right track," Sheraton smiled. "I just didn't think that Barbara would be the first one we would get to question. She's a difficult one."

"Let's hope we'll have some beginners luck," Jeremy smiled back. "We should have started with Jazz but, fate dealt us a bad hand and we got stuck with...Oh. Hello Barbara. You're back."

"I am so surprised," Barbara said, lowering herself into the straight backed chair. "They actually have indoor plumbing. Considering the fact that this place is decorated in early cave I half expected that, when I asked for directions to the ladies room, they were going to hand me a shovel and open up the back door and point me toward the yard."

"They only save that privilege for V.I.P's," Jeremy said.

Jeremy leaned his chair back against a sand colored tapestry that was loosely hanging from the wall behind him. "You have to try the ribs here. They prepare them with a special sauce."

"That sounds like a real hoot," Barbara announced, drinking thirstily from her drink. "I'm sure my orthodontist will just love having to pull pieces of a dead water buffalo out from between my teeth."

Barbara pulled out a small mirror and studied herself. Then, she opened her purse and pulled out a variety of tubes and sticks and began to make her face up."

"I don't know if Jeremy or I had the chance yet," Sheraton said. "But, we are sorry that Gene is dead." He felt that it was close enough to the truth so that he hadn't lied but would still give Barbara the feeling that he was offering her compassion. "It must have been awful."

"Yeah. It was a real bitch." Barbara was so intent on putting on her fresh make-up that she didn't pause in her cosmetic mini-surgery as she spoke. "What kind of meat do they put in their chili, rattlesnake?"

Jeremy asked, "Why? Does your dentist charge extra to extract rattlesnake meat from between your teeth?"

"How the hell are we suppose to order food if they don't send a waitress over to our table," Barbara complained. "Or, is she stuck at some other table having to read the menu out to somebody. The patrons here can read and write, can't they?"

"They read and they write," Jeremy told her. "That is, they read and write when they're not all too busy out rustling cattle or trying to spark the local school marm."

Barbara put the lid back on a tube of lip gloss. "I thought that maybe they just had a cattle drive walk past the tables and everybody would point to what they wanted for an entree."

"Be nice when the waitress does come around," Jeremy suggested. "She carries a sawed off shot gun and uses it when the mood strikes her."

"For all I care, she can douche with the damn thing," Barbara snapped. The one drink, very strong, was having an immediate effect on her. Jeremy signaled for a refill all around.

"I just want to order something that won't taste as if it's something Hopalong Cassidy uses to polish his boots with," Barbara complained. "I'm a classy broad. I'm not use to drinking from dirty glasses."

"That's salt around the rim of your glass," Sheraton said, explaining a Margarita to Barbara.

"Salt? Do they expect me to take a bite out of the glass if I get too hungry? Honestly. Gene would turn in his grave if he knew I was in a cheap joint like this."

"I'm sure you and Gene salted a few rims in your time," Jeremy said to her.

"It was nice that Gene found somebody," Sheraton said. "He was always alone. I'm glad he had a lover."

Barbara seemed disturbed. "What am I suppose to say if our waitress, Miss Kitty probably, asks me how I like this shit? Am I suppose to let out a big, 'yahoo' or give her the old spread eagle?"

"We'll give her a nice, old silver dollar and that should make the little lady pleased," Jeremy grinned.

"Maybe she can use it to buy some barbed wire to put over her front teeth. Honestly. One of them reaches almost all the way to Oklahoma."

"Were you and Gene close with Jazz?" Sheraton felt that Barbara's insults weren't going to be easy to ignore or pass around so he tried a direct approach.

Barbara didn't answer immediately. Instead, she pulled into her bag again and started to redo her make-up.

"Why didn't you do that in the ladies room?" Jeremy asked.

"Because I saw a beer bottle in there," she snapped. "I have a feeling it was for the customers to use."

Jeremy, who would have liked nothing better than to tell Barbara what she could do with a beer bottle, gritted his teeth until they were clenched uncomfortably tight.

"It was nice of you trying to see Jazz today," Sheraton continued.

"Are you sure the food here doesn't directly effect the central nervous system?" Barbara asked, ignoring Sheraton as much as it was possible. "Look what it's done to some of the patrons."

"If it does, Barbara, I'm sure nobody will notice the difference," Jeremy said. "Now, did you get up to see Jazz?"

"If I order an enchilada will the chef have to have Trigger back into a Cusinart first?"

"Stop ignoring the question."

"I just want to finish lunch before the afternoon stampede," Barbara cried.

"Barbara, do you think that Jazz killed Gene?"

"He could have," she said almost as simply as the other people in the room ordered their entrees. "Lord knows he was as infatuated with Gene as possible. And, jealous as hell."

"Jealous?" Sheraton said it mildly but, for some odd reason, something was hitting a sour note with him.

"He knew how Gene felt about me," Barbara said.

"I thought that was some state secret," Sheraton said.

"Only from people like you and Jeremy who never had the decency to call Gene up from time to time to see how he was. The others, people like Jazz and a few others, had to find out."

"Gene told them?"

"Not exactly," she said. "He didn't tell anybody."

"Then how would they have found out?" Jeremy asked.

"By dropping by uninvited," Barbara replied.

"You mean, friends dropped by?" Jeremy asked. "Like Karen?"

"Please!" Barbara screamed. "I am eating."

"Did she know about you and Gene?" Sheraton persisted.

"Karen?" Barbara choked with laughter. "You had to see that desperate broad. Knocking on the door and begging for my man to let her in and love her. It was so pathetic. Sometimes I wanted to come out of the bathroom where Gene always made me hide just to see the look on her face and really give her something to talk about." Barbara laughed but then stopped shortly. "Why? What is she saying now?"

"Oh," Jeremy mused. "Nothing much. Just about how lonely Gene was and how he needed some good loving."

Barbara seemed to relax. "I suppose she has her version of how my beloved died?"

"Not really," Sheraton informed Barbara. "She did say about how much Gene changed toward the end. Of course, being you were Gene's woman, you know that already."

"You don't seriously think I'm going to agree to anything that miserable bitch says, do you?"

Sheraton looked serious. "Karen seemed pretty certain of her facts."

"The last time that cow had a pap test, the gynecologist found a brain tumor. You can't believe her."

Sheraton leaned over and scattered some of his rice on his plate. "That's why we're asking you these questions, Barbara. So we can find out what really happened to our friend."

Barbara missed the flattery. She was too busy in her complaints to notice. "Karen talks about Gene changing. How would she know about change? She's too busy reading up about menopause to prepare herself for the biggest thrill she'll probably ever have in her life.

"Gene and I were in love. Karen wouldn't know about that. Fags wouldn't understand it either. It wasn't just fucking and sucking; it was real love."

"Ah, Barbara," Jeremy said. "You may be a woman but you still talk like a Camp Fire Girl."

Now, well into her third drink, Barbara was dizzy and feeling no pain. When Sheraton asked her, "You mean Karen lied?" She seemed to be almost expecting it.

"Karen's an old, ugly witch. She bothered Gene because she had this crazy idea that he could easily get his hands on drugs. She needed something to relieve the boredom of those long nights without a real man to love her."

"You mean Marty?" Sheraton stopped before finishing.

"You think that worm is a man? You like men. Think about it. He was as hot and horny for Gene as that slime of his wife was."

"Gene told you that?" Sheraton asked.

"Forget it," Barbara snarled. "Just forget it. He's gone. What does it matter? All that matters is that the stupid waitress should stop soul kissing Deputy Dawg and get her ass here and take our drink order. Mine is all gone."

"Gene," Jeremy said as he signaled for another drink-only for Barbara. "Gene wasn't doing drugs then?"

"Baby," she said, leaning over the table and letting her large, clumsy jewelry clank against the table. "I was his drug."

Barbara snapped out her drink order and then turned venomous eyes on the duo.

"What did that bitch say about me anyway?"

"Oh," Jeremy smiled. "Just about what a great gal you were and how she missed those long nights when you and she use to play *Uno* together."

"Little prick!"

"Barbara. Please. I have a reputation to maintain in this neighborhood."

"I was referring to Marty," she nobly said. "But, do feel free to take it personally."

"You don't like either of them, do you?"

"No Jeremy, I do not. Surprised? Well, they laughed at me and, when Gene turned them both out of his bed, I had the last laugh."

Jeremy nodded and tipped his glass to drain it. "I guess, Sheraton, we can cross out what Karen told us from that list of yours."

"What list?" Barbara said.

"Just playing Dick Tracy," Jeremy said.

"You got the 'Dick' part right." Not even the fresh drink in front of her mollified Barbara now. "You actually believed a woman who's wardrobe is funnier than a Neil Simon comedy? Why, that woman is just a desperate hussy.

"You had to hear that fat assed vixen begging Gene for sex. I was standing in his bathroom-that's where he kept his mop. Why, I had never seen one before and I wouldn't know what to do with one! It's a good thing Gene loved me for my bitching body and not my domestic skills.

"Anyway, Gene turned down all her desperate advances. She was pathetic. He didn't want her and he as much as told her so."

Barbara, sensing that the fun was over, rose to leave.

"At least now we know that Karen was only exaggerating," Sheraton said swiftly.

"Exaggerating?" Barbara screamed. "Try bald faced lying."

"She made it sound as if she were Gene's lover and slave," Sheraton said.

"He didn't give her the time of day," Barbara said, woozy in her movements now. "Unless you consider the fact that he almost told her where to go, he never had anything to do with her. That you can take from me."

*   *   *

Barbara made every attempt at leaving. Considering the fact that the elaborate and bountiful meal that she had ordered had yet to be delivered, it made Sheraton even more determined in his belief that she was hiding something.

"Sit down," Jeremy said, yanking her arm and letting the bulky jewelry clang out several choruses of a tune.

"Why?" Her eyes were cloudy and the drinks she had consumed had already gotten the best of her. Weaving slowly back and forth, she seemed more angry than confused or scared.

"You don't believe a word that I've been telling you," she said, slipping into the seat again. Gone was a good amount of the over glossed surface that she had varnished herself with for the lunch. In it's place was a nasty, foul mooded woman who was determined to do battle with them.

"You can't blame us much," Sheraton said gently enough so as not to disturb her any more than she already was. "You and Gene were hardly friendly toward each other."

"That was then. It was different at the end. He wanted me."

Sheraton, positive that if Gene wanted Barbara there had to be an ulterior motive, mildly put his questions to her.

"Did he want you to do anything for him?"

"What is this?" A good deal of the cocky, self assurance crept back into the woman. "Do you want to hear about all the sordid details of our love life? Is that what this is all about?"

"What do you think it's about, Barbara?"

Slyly, with a craftiness that they had forgotten, Barbara began to speak to them in a dry, vulgar way.

"I thought that maybe you wanted to be friends with me. I thought that now, in my hour of need, you were kind and human enough to actually care about another person."

"We care enough about you to want to know the truth," Jeremy said. "What did happen to Gene? Do you know?"

"Look. I told you. He was a sweet, honest guy who was really shy and lonesome."

"And then you came along and turned his life around for him?"

"He was practically a hermit," Barbara said. "He didn't go any-where or do anything. He just sat in that dreadful apartment of his all day and all night."

"Why?" Sheraton asked. "He was still young. He wasn't chained to one of the walls. Why didn't he go out and socialize?"

A bit of concern and confusion swallowed up much of Barbara's hostilities. "I don't know. I just know that he didn't go out. People had to come and see him."

"Was he afraid to go out?"

Barbara looked at Sheraton. "You mean like one of those phobia's where a person is scared of the wide, open spaces?"

Jeremy shook his head. "I mean like the fear a person gets when he's crossed one too many people and he knows that they may be out to get him for something."

"I don't know," Barbara said, putting her hands on her glass but not drinking from it. A quietude fell over her and seemed to play upon her words. "He was a difficult person to get to know."

"Difficult how?" Sheraton wanted to know. "Difficult as in he was argumentative?"

"He was a fighter," she said. "But that isn't what I mean. He was difficult to know. Real weird sometimes. It was hard to figure him out.

"You're right. He did hate me at once. Recently, that changed. He treated me right."

Sheraton listened for a while and then asked, "You mean he was kind and considerate toward you?"

"He was OK," she answered, seeming as if she wanted to explain that further but hesitated in doing so. "Like I said, it was hard to get to know him."

"Could he have been on drugs or something?"

Barbara snapped her fingers and a waitress, tired and over-worked, came rushing over to take her drink order.

After ordering, Barbara said: "Why is it every time someone is quiet or not totally responsive, some clown asks if they're doing drugs. Honestly. Once it was diarrhea. Then constipation. Now it's drugs.

"Not everybody is a junkie! I don't think the man bought food, never mind buying drugs."

"Drugs," Jeremy told her, "might explain his dark moods and his attitude."

"Were you turned on by him too?" she asked suddenly.

"You mean, did he try to sell us drugs?"

"Damn you, Jeremy. I mean, were you sexually attracted to him like Karen was. Or that stupid Jazz. Did you want to get him into bed like the others did?"

"No. Did you?"

As if she hadn't heard the question, Barbara said: "Even that dolt Marty acted as if he wanted Gene to give him his sorority pin."

"How about Gene's brother, Alan?" Sheraton slipped the name in during one of Barbara's more pensive moments. "Did he and Gene get along that well together?"

"They hated each other," she said. "Gene didn't like Alan to come around but that didn't stop baby brother. He was always on the door step. Always preaching and arguing with Gene."

"About what?"

Barbara's eyes shot up like flares that had been ignited.

"About great deals and about money. Alan is a bum. He doesn't want to work but he certainly loves to party. It takes money to do that."

Sheraton looked surprised. Somehow, diminutive Alan didn't strike him as a party animal.

"He thought that Gene was going to give him money?" Barbara nodded and Sheraton went on with the questioning. "Where was Gene suppose to get the money to give Alan when he didn't have it for himself?"

"Alan has these schemes and wild ideas. Ask him if you're both so damned interested."

Sheraton was interested. "They fought?"

"Alan fought. He has a filthy temper and he was constantly upsetting Gene."

"Was Jazz around when Alan was arguing with Gene?"

"Where do you think they argued, Madison Square Garden? It wasn't exactly something that you would send out invitations to."

Patting her hand as he spoke, Sheraton said: "But Jazz did know Alan and all about the arguments, didn't he?"

"He knew but..."

Barbara snapped her head up. "You son of a bitch."

"What do you know, Barbara?" Jeremy was past being polite. He demanded an answer and practically shouted out the question.

"Go to hell. Both of you."

"You loved Gene," Sheraton said. "Why won't you do anything to see that his killer is caught?"

"Maybe he has been caught," she hinted. "Maybe he's caught and the police already have him. Maybe I tried to see him today so that I could spit in his face."

"And maybe not," Jeremy said.

Barbara leaned across the table, her elaborate necklace scraping the top of the table. "Unless you did it, maybe you're wrong. Maybe the cops already have the bastard."

"You know this for a fact?"

Abruptly Barbara swung into a softer mood. "I don't know anything. In fact, I bet I know just as much-or as little, whatever the case may be-as you know."

Sheraton smiled wanly while Jeremy told her, "And maybe you're wrong."

NINE

Behind them, a jazz pianist played a light, bouncy medley. Waitresses hopped and bopped-dinner trays of steak and baked potatoes apparently having been glued onto their arms. The whole atmosphere was dark, surprisingly smoke free and looked as if the whole joint was just preparing for the moment when somebody pulled a switch and starting the place jumping.

"This is nice," Pris said, as she looked around the place-*Fat Tuesday's*-and found herself an instant convert to jazz.

"I like it," Alan said to no one in particular. Behind glasses that had lenses tinted to darkly they might be black, he seemed an ominous figure indeed.

Jeremy, who had allowed Sheraton to persuade him into entertaining (and picking up the tab) for both lunch and dinner, seemed contingently docile about it.

"Jazz," Pris said, wondering if anyone else had made the same connection. "Why, it's something I never even thought about before tonight."

"Really?" Alan seemed convinced that keeping on dark glasses in a dark room was a crowning achievement to his border line good looks. "What kind of music are you into?"

Pris, playing a part for Sheraton that she hadn't rehearsed, tried to recoup herself admirably. "Chamber music mostly. Or, old Ukrainian dirges. Anything that I can snap my fingers to while I'm listening."

Roughly cutting off a large chunk of steak and shoving it first into a pool of steak sauce and then his mouth, Alan nodded absently while he tried to follow the beat.

"That's wild. Yeah. Real crazy."

"Good lord," Sheraton thought. "This man is on dope. Or trying to give a darn good impression that he is."

"But today," Pris continued, "it seems that all I hear about is jazz. First that friend of yours, Alan. Now this."

"Friend?" Alan picked up a stein of beer and quickly washed a stuck piece of meat down his throat.

"Jazz," Pris smiled. "Tall, blonde and wears shoes that match his purse. I dare say you can pick him out in a crowd."

"My brothers friend," Alan replied, relaxing and getting back into the mood of the music again.

Sheraton had spent some time and a great deal of effort on tracking down Alan. Getting his number from his distraught mother was a long, drawn-out process. He wasn't going to allow the man to palm off answers casually.

"Jazz told us that the two of you met one night."

"Me and Jazz?" Alan stuck out his index finger and roughly shoved the sunglasses up the bridge of his nose.

"I thought that was you," Pris said, clapping her hands as if she were delighted with a sudden recollection. "Standing outside the Duchess the other night."

"Is that a jazz club or is that the place you go to hear some of your Slavic funeral tunes?"

"Neither actually. It's a woman's bar in the Village. But, you already know that, don't you?"

Though they couldn't make out his eyes through the dark glasses, all were sure that Alan was glaring at them.

"I met Jazz on the street. I was walking around the Village." Alan stopped and dropped a dollop of sour cream onto his baked potato.

He did it with too much physical energy attached to the action and some spattered on the red checked table cloth. "I was trying to walk away from my problems. My brothers death-that was a real bummer."

Jeremy slid some vegetables around his plate. "I haven't heard that word used since the last time I went to a love-in...Or was it a be-in? I always use to get the two confused."

Sheraton smiled. "He makes one heck of a pal but he was a lousy hippie."

"Look," Alan said, sliding back his plate although he hadn't hardly touched the bulk of the food on it yet. "I'm really fried over this thing with my brother. I just can't handle it and I definitely don't want to talk about it."

"Why?" Sheraton asked as the pianist stopped for a round of hearty applause.

"Because it hurts," Alan said. "It hurts like hell."

"Forgive me, Alan, but you and Gene weren't that close."

"We had our differences," the man allowed. "They weren't major ones but they did put a strain on us at times."

"At times?" Jeremy coughed dryly. "You didn't shed a tear at your brothers funeral and you were too busy following us to attend any wake afterward or to be with your family."

"I was lonesome. I needed some company."

Sheraton nudged his mouth into a smile. "Was your need for company so great that you tracked down Jazz-the person, not the music form-to find some?"

"Nobody could be that lonesome," Alan declared. "I didn't exactly track him down either. As your friend said, you could spot him in a crowd.

"I was curious about Jazz. Not the whole transvestite thing. To me that's all bull. Men dress up like women because that's the only way they think they can attract a guy."

"Imagine the psychiatrists surprise when your report is published in the next medical journal," Pris sighed.

"My brother may have liked guys dressing like women but I don't," Alan said, speaking as if he desperately needed to be believed. "I also don't trust Jazz-even from the little I've seen of him. What the hell was he doing hanging around my brother all the time? If you knew anything about Gene then you must have known how he felt about gays."

"I think we have some of his choicer words crocheted on a pillow at home," Jeremy said. "For the record, Jazz was dealing for your brother."

"Dealing? You mean drugs?"

"Your brother wasn't running a casino. Of course I mean drugs. And, don't bother to get a soap box and declare how anti-drugs you are. Not with the shape those eyes must be under those glasses."

"You think I'm stoned?" Alan spoke blustery words but he made no move to take off the glasses to prove Jeremy wrong.

Sheraton told him, "What you do is your business. Right now, we'd like to know why you hate Jazz so much. Also, do you think he really killed your brother?"

Alan slid his plate back in front of him again. Sheraton wondered if he was going to use eating as an excuse not to talk but Alan was versatile enough to do both.

"My brother mentioned something that makes me think that Jazz was getting out of hand with him. You do know that Jazz was infatuated with my brother, don't you?"

"It seems that the city was struck with an epidemic of people who had the hots for Gene," Jeremy said.

"Well, Gene really blew off some steam about Jazz. I didn't know about his dealing. I mean, I knew he was wasted half the time. One night, he was pretty far gone and he told me about how he hated the whole cross-dressing thing. He used some pretty strong terms for it," he said, looking at Pris.

"You can feel free to repeat them if you think it's necessary," she said. "I'm a pretty strong lady."

"You know the stuff he said. That isn't important. What is important is that he felt that it was going too far and he couldn't stop or control Jazz any longer."

"Gene really told you that?" Sheraton asked.

"Man," Alan said, attacking the steak with his knife and fork. "He really cut loose. He told me how sick he was of all the fruits and sickies who thought that because they put on a dress they could fall into his bed. He was sick of the whole scene. Maybe, if what you're saying is true, he allowed Jazz over because he wanted somebody to push the stuff for him. I think that Jazz might have gotten the wrong impression and really put the make on my brother. You know how weird he got when somebody tried to get close to him or even touch him."

"So, you think Jazz tried to seduce Gene?" Pris asked.

"Yeah. I do."

"Then why was your brother found wearing only his underwear?" Sheraton asked. "If he lacked sexual interest in Jazz-or anyone else-why try to ward off their advances while he was half undressed?"

"I don't know about that. Maybe Jazz tried to rape him."

"Come off it," Jeremy snapped. "You have to see how stupid that sounds."

"My brother was pretty adamant about transvestites," Alan said. "He might have allowed Jazz some extra leeway like using his bathroom to put all that crap on his face and such but he wouldn't have sex with him."

Sheraton fumbled with an idea and tried to say it without a blush. "How about teasing someone? Would Gene pretend to come on to somebody?"

Alan's silence was an indication that Sheraton's idea wasn't wild or far fetched.

"That would explain why Gene didn't have his pants on," Pris pointed out.

"It would also put your friend Jazz right back into the hot seat," Alan answered evenly.

"Jazz is in the hospital now," Sheraton told Alan. "He tried to kill himself after he was arrested."

"We tried to see him but couldn't," Jeremy added.

"You went to the hospital and tried to see him?" Alan said loudly.

"No. I went to the hospital because I wanted to play Penny Sunkist and bring him his orange juice. Of course we wanted to see him. Why? Wouldn't you want to speak to him?"

Alan picked up his napkin and threw it down over his plate. "Of course. But, not to prove he was innocent. I want to prove that he is guilty.

"You see, I feel much the same way my brother did. He told me how much he hated fags in dresses and so do I. I don't want to see Jazz to be his friend. I want to murder him."

*   *   *

Jeremy fought off an uncontrollable desire to take away Sheraton's American Express card.

"Either it's that or I'm going to burn your date book," he said to the back of Sheraton's head.

"So long as you leave me my computer." Above the clacking of the keys, Sheraton was busily typing something into a big blue box situated roughly in the middle of a colorful screen.

"I don't have to guess what you're doing now." Jeremy was walking around the apartment, a toothbrush and foamy bubbles pouring out of his mouth as he spoke. "You're either making up a profile of Alan or amending the one you already have."

It was with such a certainty that Jeremy spoke that when he beetled his neck over Sheraton's shoulder, he was quite surprised as what he saw on the screen.

"You're writing about Gene?" That was the last name that Jeremy expected to see compiled in the database of facts.

"I think the problem with us is that we didn't know Gene at all."

"From all I've heard about, I can't say that I'm too sorry that we missed the chance to get to know him better. It's costly enough treating his girl friend and brother to expensive meals without having to have paid him blackmail money to boot."

"The blackmailing angle is only one part of it," Sheraton said, speaking as he typed. "It's the whole personality of the man that I think we should be investigating.

"Who was he? What motivated him like that? Did you ever stop to wonder about hatred, Jeremy?"

"I'm too busy disliking the entire world to take time out to think about it."

"You know what I mean. Why did Gene hate gay's so much?"

"I'm sure that somewhere, somebody is going to claim that Gene was sexually abused by his Scout Master when he was just a boy. Maybe the Boy Scout's should start selling cookies. It would give them a better image in the public's mind."

A small candle flickered at one end of the apartment. It cast a cozy, warm glow over the room.

"Sometimes," Sheraton said, "when a person protests too much about any given subject, it always makes me suspicious."

"Since you got on this investigating kick of yours, you're suspicious of everything. I swear I saw you trying to lift fingerprints off the milk carton this morning."

"How about the way that people perceived Gene?" Sheraton was serious now; serious enough to take a break from typing in data and to turn to look at Jeremy. His eyes flickered like sparkling highlights from the glowing candle.

"I know that different people see us in all sorts of ways but it seems that almost everybody had this romantic image of Gene fixed in their minds. That's odd because, by all reports, Gene was one step beyond asexual."

"The attraction then was the thrill of the hunt and the challenge," Jeremy said. "Imagine how much more I'd love you if you had put up a struggle."

"We touched on something tonight."

"I was hoping we could do a lot of touching tonight if you'd only turn off that bloody computer and come to bed."

"Jeremy, do you think Gene played games?"

Images of carnal bliss floated as far away as notions of Nirvana for Jeremy.

"I think he played with people's minds if you want to know the truth. I believe that Gene was so hooked on drugs that he seduced innocent and frustrated people like Jazz and Karen so that they'd do his dirty work for him."

"You mean, make them think that if they made him happy by selling drugs for him then he'd make them happy?"

"Sounds real cheap, doesn't it?"

Sheraton started to turn back to the screen but stopped. A certain grade of interest was knocked out of him now.

"It also could be made into a credible case against one of the people who Gene tried to fool. Get them so disgusted with both him and themselves when they realized that they had been used that they got angry with Gene. But, could somebody like Jazz get angry enough to kill a man?"

"Honestly?" Jeremy seemed sure of his answer. "No. But I can't say the same for Karen. I don't mean that she's Jack the Ripper's distaff partner. It's just that you hear so much about a woman scorned."

"Then we'd have to put Barbara's name before Karen's."

"I'm sure Karen would love playing second fiddle even if it were on *that* list!"

"Barbara is either very smart or-and I do hate to say this-telling the truth. Jeremy, she didn't act like she was selling drugs or pushing them for Gene."

"Ah. But can you believe that she and Gene were having an affair?"

"I think that Gene was playing up to Barbara in hopes of adding her services to his growing drug-selling trade."

Jeremy snapped his fingers. "And then Barbara exaggerated it in her mind. She got carried away with it.

"Somebody like Karen is shrewd enough to realize, eventually, that she's playing the fool. Barbara might not be that sharp." Then, a certain amount of light went out of his voice. "However, that could still mean that when the day came that Barbara realized that Gene was just trying to use her, she sought her revenge on him for toying with her supposed affection."

"How about Marty?" Sheraton had trouble with this concept. He honestly liked the man. "He had a double hurt there. First, he might have suspected that Gene was trying to seduce his wife. Next, he might have gotten scared with Gene's threats. I just don't see Marty getting that scared that he would kill Gene."

Jeremy walked over and began to search for the switch that would turn off the computer.

"So, I guess we've taken it as far as we can for tonight. Tomorrow, the lawyer that Pris introduced us to is going to try to see if she can wangle us into visiting Jazz."

"In your murder mysteries, how are the cases generally solved?"

Jeremy's fingers stopped fumbling for the switch. "Those are books, Sheraton. Carefully plotted works that a person like Ed McBain make work because he has some control over the story line. He puts a clue somewhere in there-"

"Generally it's an innocuous item that is so everyday ordinary or mundane that it doesn't mean anything at first."

"Until the next to last chapter." Jeremy ran his fingers through Sheraton's hair and mussed it. "That's fine for Random House but not for real life."

"Suppose there was something that we missed? Don't forget, we're dealing with our friends and people we know-not hard-edged killers."

"Then you're not considering Barbara?"

"You know what I mean. Jeremy, we have to go over this and start from the beginning."

Jeremy stood up and protested. "That could take all night."

"We're both on sick leave because of our accident."

"An accident that I don't want to have repeated."

"Jeremy, we have to try. True, we might end indicting one friend but at least we'll be clearing the names of the others."

"And getting ourselves put even further into the bad graces of Detective Lawrence. Sheraton, do you really want to have to tangle with the likes of him or that half-brained partner of his again?"

"If it means that we could get Jazz out of jail, I say yes."

"I say you're crazy."

Sheraton looked at him. "But?"

"But, we're partners in this. I don't like it much but, if you're going to go ahead with it then I guess, like it or not, I'm going to be right behind you."

"Did I ever tell you I love you?"

"Yes you did. That's what's making me risk my neck for this wild idea of yours."

They worked far into the night. The candle burnt out and, in the glow of the computer screen, neither man realized it.

Around four in the morning, the desk littered with cookie crumbs and half drunk cups of cold tea, Sheraton pointed out something. It was the insipid, small fact that no one had paid any attention to-then.

TEN

Walking in the twilight hours of the next evening toward the hospital, it was all still pretty much left up in the air. Requests had been made. Requests had been denied. Petitions, begging pleas and hot arguments ensued.

Detective Lawrence, spurned into an over obnoxious bearing soul due to the continuous, close proximity of his partner Detective Stone, found that he could heartily laugh at it.

"You want me to give the two of you permission to go and talk to your friend?" He hooted again, even louder-and more vicious. "He already tried to kill himself once. What makes you think that the sight of you is going to fill him with a will to live?"

"There are things we suspect," Sheraton answered. He knew that the man was going to laugh off any logic attached to his request so he didn't go into any detail. "You could keep a man posted outside the door all the while; we've no objection to that."

"How kind of you. Perhaps while you and your friend are chatting, I can make some tea and bake you some scones."

Jeremy's forbearance was severely limited and, in the presence of these two men, it was tested sorely.

"We're not going up there to schmooze with him. We're trying to figure out just who killed a man."

"What the hell do you think the police department is trying to do? We haven't got him under constant surveillance so that our men will know what the well dressed transvestite will be wearing next spring."

"How successful have you been?" Jeremy shouted. He leaned across the man's cluttered desk. Countless Styrofoam cups of coffee had left numerous rings on the top. Nobody had bothered to clean them or, probably, never thought to do so. "Not very, right? Well, we're his friends. He might not talk to you-"

"Why not, pussycat? I'm such a warm and friendly guy."

"I think you intimidate him. It's the way you pick your teeth with the butt end of your pistol that scares them off.

"Jazz isn't afraid of Sheraton or myself. He might talk to us. Right now, you're wasting the taxpayers money."

"Is this going to be another crack about our salaries?" Detective Stone asked suspiciously.

"He was talking about the cost of the hospital room that Jazz is in," Sheraton explained. "Jeremy is right. You haven't gotten any-where fast-why not let us try?"

"Because I don't trust you anymore than I like you," Detective Lawrence said, blunt and honest to a fault.

It had occurred to Sheraton that the police department wasn't going to be too eager to go with their idea. That was why he had come to this meeting armed with patience and a determination.

"We've been thinking a lot about Gene's death," Sheraton said.

"I'm sure that keeps you off the streets at night, pussycat."

"It's all too mixed up and crazy for you to automatically pin it on Jazz."

"You call proof that Gene had tried to fight off Jazz a hunch?" Detective Lawrence looked at Detective Stone. "We've got him dead to rights."

"If he's go guilty, why hasn't he confessed then?" Jeremy said.

"He hasn't exactly been straining his vocal chords-as sweet as they may be-to proclaim how innocent he is either." Detective Stone's little present to them had been unexpected.

"Don't you think that with the fear of being in prison along with the drugs they must have pumped into him at the hospital that he would have said something by now?"

"Look," Detective Lawrence said as he shoved his hands into the top of his pants, past the alligator belt. "I've met killers, have either of you?"

"Yes," Jeremy said. "It's an almost automatic fact that we must know Gene's killer. After all, weren't you the one who pointed out the fact that Gene knew his killer? He hadn't been going around making new pals so it was just the same, old gang he always hung around with."

Detective Stone snorted. "Including you two. If we're compiling lists of suspects other than Jazz than you have to include your names."

"Except that we can alibi each other," Sheraton pointed out in an uncaring way.

"Tell me this," Detective Lawrence asked. "If your pal is so damn innocent, why did he try to kill himself?"

"Because he's scared," Sheraton said. "He knows he didn't kill Gene. I also think that he knows who did kill him."

A ruffled flurry of interest shot over Detective Lawrence's face. Sheraton played on it.

"You don't know Jazz. You see a man who is interested in putting on cosmetics and a dress. Yes. That's a part of the man but there's a lot more to Jazz than that."

"We know, pussycat. Remember, we strip searched him."

"You know what we mean," Jeremy shouted. "He's a sensitive kid who's not too swift on the up-take at times. Under the pressure he was suffering through he probably got so confused that he hit the panic button. Despite it all, he's not dumb."

"Never said he was," Detective Stone said. "His eye shadow always matches the blouse he's wearing."

"He's sensitive and he's scared to face the truth," Sheraton told them. "He knows things that he isn't talking about just now."

"Why?" Both asked.

"Maybe you haven't asked him the right questions," Jeremy said. "Maybe you've all been so bloody busy treating him like a sick faggot that you haven't bothered to look past the clothes and the wigs to treat him as a normal, adjusted person. His wearing a dress is no sicker than your choice in wearing that tie with that shirt."

Both men stared at their neckwear.

"Let us just ask him a few questions," Sheraton pleaded. "It couldn't hurt. You've already made your minds up so what can be the harm?"

"It's against regulations," Detective Stone recited in his best text book manner.

"So is sending an innocent man to jail," Jeremy informed him.

"We've got another problem," Detective Lawrence said, speaking both to them and into the phone receiver he was holding. "That stupid drag queen escaped from the hospital."

"He what?" Detective Stone shouted angrily.

"How could he?" Sheraton asked. "I thought the door was guarded."

"It was but he managed to escape," Detective Lawrence said, pulling on his jacket. "We've got to get right over there, partner."

"So do we," Jeremy said to Sheraton. "Come on, partner."

A beehive flurrying of activity was going on in the dimly lit central hall of the hospital when Jeremy and Sheraton arrived there. More for moral support than idle curiosity, Pris had tagged along with them.

Detective Lawrence, somber and gravely voiced, shouted out orders while he ignored the impatient stares of the doctors and nurses who tried to maintain some semblance of a hospital atmosphere while blue uniformed officers rushed around the place.

"What happened exactly?" Sheraton heard Detective Stone ask a flustered orderly.

The orderly who was being questioned was pale, wan and had a nature that made him fidgety and jumpy at the first sign of trouble. He was not the sort of person who should be questioned in Detective Stone's peculiarly harassing way.

"He was in his room. There was a guard on the door."

"We know that, pussycat," Detective Lawrence shouted from across the room while a flock of steel lipped nurses watched the man in appalled silence. "Our men don't make mistakes. He was at that door always."

Sheraton, knowing full well that he would get his head bitten off for asking a question now but proceeding anyway said: "Excuse me but why are you questioning this man?"

In his anger, Detective Lawrence didn't stop to think about who was asking the question before he answered. "Because, right before that killer escaped from his room, this clown went into his room and spent an awfully long time there serving him his dinner."

Jeremy exchanged a glance first with Pris and then Sheraton. An idea was quickly forming in their minds. Crazy as it seemed, a sort of telepathy was working. Notions were entering their heads and, looking at each other with sideways glances, they each would have sworn that they were thinking the same thing.

The orderly, sweaty now and yanking at the collar of his loose fitting white jacket, seemed ready to pass out on the floor.

"Jeremy," Sheraton whispered. "Are you thinking what I'm thinking?"

"It's the earring," Jeremy said in a hushed voice. "I can't tell anymore. I think if my grandfather was still alive, he'd have one on too."

"He's gay," Pris said, joining in on the private discussion. "You think it's possible that he helped Jazz escape?"

"But how?" Sheraton felt that the orderly had a nervous streak in him that went far beyond just being frightened at having to be questioned by the police. His Adam's apple was bobbing up and down as if he were trying to ingest words he hadn't told the police.

Finally, after two police officers with walkie talkies approached Detective Lawrence, Sheraton and Jeremy cornered the young man.

"Look," he said in a whining voice. "I don't know anything."

"You also don't want to lose your job," Sheraton soothingly said. "We're not going to get you in trouble. I have a feeling that you feel about Jazz-the man they're looking for right now-just the same way that we do. We're trying to help him."

"He was a good kid," the orderly said, brushing back damp strands of slate colored hair from his forehead. A pimply brow was revealed. "He only wanted to dress up and have some fun."

"We know," Sheraton said, fighting off the urge to grip the man and shake the story out of him. "How did you know? Did Jazz talk to you?"

"He said things," the man admitted. "I don't know if it was the sedatives they gave him or what but he talked incoherently. That wasn't like him."

An explosion of light went off inside Jeremy's head. "You knew Jazz before you saw him here at the hospital?"

"I didn't say that."

"Look. We're not the cops. We're friends of Jazz."

"I saw him around. In the clubs and on the street." Getting only that much of the story out of the young man was tough work. Sheraton wondered what it would take to get the rest of it out.

Jeremy, trying to filter away the lapsed moments that it would take to get the orderly to admit his hand in the escape, gave him a plausible explanation of what might have happened in Jazz's room. If it were false, he felt sure that the orderly would correct the information.

"You went in the room and recognized Jazz. You knew him from the streets. Maybe you have a sensitive understanding of drag queens and you can sympathize with them.

"So, you went into his room this afternoon to give him his dinner."

"His hands were restrained," the orderly gasped, sounding as if he had just run a ten kilometer race. "I had to feed him."

"Did Jazz recognize you?"

The orderly nodded. "He told me he was scared. He couldn't talk about what happened to that guy who they're trying to say he killed. I do know that he loved him. I don't think Jazz could kill anyone-especially somebody he was crazy about."

"You took off the restraining straps," Sheraton said, speaking gently and informally. It wouldn't do to scare the man anymore than he already was. "You helped a friend. There's no crime in that."

"There would be if that guy who keeps calling me 'pussycat' were to hear about it."

"Forget about Detective Lawrence," Jeremy ordered him. "After you took off the straps, what happened?"

"I hid Jazz under the cart where we put the trays of food for the patients. It was easier than it sounds; Jazz had that snake hipped figure that I envied. Try as I might, I can't loose these hips of mine and—"

"We'll sign you up for *Nutri-Systems* in the morning," Jeremy exclaimed. "Right now, tell us what happened after you hid Jazz. After you wheeled him out of the room, where did he go?"

"That's just it. I don't know." The man looked at them with small, teary eyes. "There's a certain trick into getting that damn cart into the elevator. You can tip the whole thing over if you don't do it correctly. I had to take it real slow. I couldn't let that guard at the door get suspicious. I had to put on a show for him. Luckily I'm an actor at heart. Why, if they were ever to start making those great, old M-G-M musicals again, I bet I could get a part in them."

Jeremy felt a frustrated urge than was hard to quell. "Before you put your footprints into wet cement at *Grauman's Chinese Theater*, what happened next?"

If the orderly was unhappy because Jeremy, Sheraton and Pris didn't want to hear about his aspirations for the silvery screen, he didn't show it. He leaned back against the sickly green painted wall and seemed as if he were on the verge of collapse.

"That's just it. I had to leave the cart unattended for a few minutes. Some old broad on that floor poked her head out of the door and started screaming for water. What do I look like, Cherry Ames? I'm not exactly Laraine Day in the old *Doctor Kildare* movies-"

"We'll give you a membership in a video club and you can sit at home nights and knock yourself out," Jeremy cried. "Just tell us what happened."

"After I got the old bitch her water-and I had to pour it for her as well-I slowly wheeled the cart down the hall. It seemed lighter to me somehow but I was afraid somebody might be watching and I didn't want to blow the whole thing.

"When I got to the elevator, I knew I could check on Jazz without anybody catching on to us. It was then that I realized that Jazz was no longer hiding."

"Where did he go?" Pris asked only to have the orderly shrug his shoulders.

"Where could he have gone off to," Sheraton asked. "Could he have sneaked off and taken the elevator down before you got out of the ladies room?"

"No. I mean, you've seen the hospital pajama's. They're a free peep show. You couldn't walk around in them and you couldn't walk down and out through the front door wearing them."

"How about going up?"

"The guard would have seen him. He would have had to," the orderly explained. "It was a long way from the old bat's room to the elevator."

"What was near the old bat's room then?" Pris asked.

"Just other rooms," he said before pausing. A strange light filled his eyes. "And the emergency steps."

"Doesn't an alarm go off when you open that door?" Jeremy quickly said.

"Usually it does. But we're doing construction and renovation work here. The alarm is off."

"So then Jazz could have walked down the steps," Sheraton said before realizing something. Jazz still couldn't have gotten out through the lobby without somebody seeing him.

"The doors on this level and in the basement are bolted," the orderly said.

Jeremy tried to think. Logically, one would go down stairs. But, if you couldn't go down, what could you do but go up.

"How about the roof?" Jeremy asked. "Jazz couldn't go down but would the roof door be open?"

"It might," the orderly replied. "They've been working up there all week. Hey," he snapped his fingers and then seemed alarmed that he might have drawn attention to himself. He quickly put his hands behind him. "The roof door is open. I heard two, hunky construction workers talking about it."

"What do we do now?" Pris asked her friends.

"What else can we do," Sheraton said. "We go up to the roof."

Pris didn't know Sheraton that well. She had assumed that in most situations he could play the peace maker, the determined soul or the arbitrator. What she didn't know was just how resolute he could be in any of these areas, especially when he was playing up the determined soul part of his character.

"Jeremy, we'll rush up the stairs while the police are milling about in confused circles."

"There must be a hundred police officers here," Jeremy said, looking at the blue swarms standing on guard all over the first floor. "How are we suppose to discreetly walk past them to the fire steps when they're not even letting visitors upstairs?"

"Pris," Sheraton beseeched, "can you think of something?"

"I knew it would come to this. My one and only chance to play the femme fatale."

"Sheraton wanted me to play that part," Jeremy told her. Then, seriously, he added: "I think you could cause a disturbance and distract what looks like the entire New York City Police Department."

"Why not ask the orderly?" Pris joked. "Why do I get the feeling that he was just born to saunter over and drop a hankie?"

Getting past the police officers was a lot easier than any of them might have imagined. Visitors, armed with bunches of flowers and boxes of candy, were heaped together in angry throngs as they waved visitor passes at the baby faced officers. Doctors and nurses, disturbed by the rough house treatment that they had to endure, were clearly on the visitors side and Detective Lawrence, always destined to be his own worse enemy, didn't make matters any better for the boys in blue by calling everyone, "pussycat" as he rigorously pushed himself through the crowds.

In such a hectic atmosphere, Sheraton and Jeremy found it almost child play easy to slip to the stairwell. True to the orderly's words, the alarm system had been disabled temporarily. The door, Jeremy realized after it swung shut, could only be opened from the outside now. Pris, who had remained on the ground floor, would have to patiently wait for their knock to release them.

Hopefully, Jeremy prayed as he winded his ways up the steep, dirty steps, it would be three people coming down these steps.

"We're on the right track," Sheraton whispered gleefully after they passed the seventh floor.

Sweating and gasping for air, Jeremy was too dizzy and too weak to wonder what his lover was talking about so Sheraton pointed to the next flight of steps going upwards.

"Foot prints," he said. "Bare foot prints. Jazz wouldn't have been wearing shoes."

"Not flats at any rate."

"He did come up here. Jeremy, he's on the roof."

"Sheraton, are you sure this is a good idea? I mean, he's not crazy but Jazz is definitely disturbed. Bloody hell, so am I."

"Come on," Sheraton insisted as he almost leaped up the next flight of steps. "I know we're doing the right thing. Jazz is up there and he needs us."

"I'm glad this is a hospital," Jeremy said, a pain filling both his knees from the climbing. "I think I'm going to have to end up in traction after this is over."

Cool winds that seldom seemed to find their way down to the street level whipped Sheraton's fine hair into his eyes. As they walked out onto the roof of the hospital, both men were too nervous and confused to accurately concentrate on anything in particular. It wasn't until then that Sheraton realized how totally unprepared they both were. The sun was rapidly going down and although the sky was a dark, golden glow with bolts of red shooting through it, they hadn't flashlights and it was rapidly getting dark.

"Sheraton," Jeremy husked in a hoarse way. "I don't see Jazz."

Both men scanned the vast circumference of the roof top. Pipes, chimneys and two large units-one for water, the other for air conditioning-were rising up over their heads and casting shadows about-deep, dark shadows looming with crevices and nooks where Jazz could hide.

They made a futile attempt at scattering themselves into running circles and whispering the man's name. Police sirens continually wailed down below and caused them to have yet another worry. Suppose the police eventually figured out that Jazz was on the roof?

"Where can he be?" Sheraton asked, his hair whipped into his eyes as he tried to peer into a shadow. The roof had a perfect panoramic view of the city but it wasn't the time to enjoy it just as it wasn't providing them with any light.

"Maybe that dumb orderly wasn't so dumb," Jeremy told him. "Maybe he helped Jazz to escape out the front door and simply decided to wave a red herring in our trail."

"You think this is all a wild goose chase?"

"Look around you. Do you see him anywhere?"

"It's a large roof," Sheraton said. "He could be hiding in a corner somewhere."

"There are a hundred buckets of tar and God knows what else all around. He could have hidden in one of them too but I don't think so, Sheraton. I think he's gone."

"He couldn't have gotten far dressed only in a hospital johnnie. No matter how liberal this part of town is, they still draw the line somewhere. Beside, how far would Jazz have gone without his make-up kit?"

Jeremy sighed at the humor in it. A man would walk around with his rear end sticking out so long as he had on his false eye lashes.

"I think the police are growing in number," Sheraton said. Another siren wailed. It was difficult to tell just how many officers were searching the building just then. "There is one thing I know; we found footsteps coming *up* the steps but not down. That has to tell you something. Jazz has got to be here someplace."

"We've looked everywhere." As if to punch his point home, Jeremy walked around and came back. "If he were *Spider Man* instead of a drag queen I'd say he was swinging from the side of the building."

"Jeremy!" A strange, excited tone had changed itself into Sheraton's voice now. "The side of the building."

"Now you've gone too far. Sheraton, do you realize what you're saying? First you had Jazz as totally innocent, then a babe in the woods and now you have him clinging to the side of a building over twelve stories above the sidewalk. What next, have him on a float at the Macy's Thanksgiving Day parade?"

Sheraton's face was glowing and he was lightly jumping up and down with excitement.

"Jeremy, the scaffolding. They're doing construction on this building."

"So? You think maybe Jazz is painting the gargoyles?"

"I think that Jazz is distraught and confused. I think that he heard the sirens and got scared and climbed over the side of the building."

Jeremy was all set to argue the point but he realized how futile it would be now. Acting again as a team, each man walked over to an opposite side of the building and peered over the side.

"I don't see anything," Jeremy complained, feeling the bitter winds of the night air cutting through him like a knife.

"Neither do I. Let's keep looking. Try calling his name."

They did that. It seemed that no matter how faintly he whispered, Sheraton's voice seemed louder than he had intended. Though, by all probability, the police on the street far below couldn't hear him, he still felt as if were giving Jazz away somehow.

"I'm cold and I'm getting very tired," Jeremy said, tucking his arms beneath the thin jacket he was wearing.

"And I'm going crazy," Sheraton said, looking out at the twinkling lights as the night time side of the city came into life. "I honestly think I see and hear Jazz everywhere."

"We've looked, honey. We've done our best. He's not here."

"He has to be here."

"Then let's throw caution to the wind," Jeremy suggested, realizing that this might be the only way to get Sheraton off the building. "Let's call Jazz: I mean really call out his name."

"Scream it?"

"What have we got to lose now? The police are going to question that orderly again eventually. As soon as they do, he'll tell them what he told us."

"Maybe not."

"The point is," Jeremy said, "we have to find him if he's up here. Don't scream your fool head off but just speak normally."

They tried it. First they ran around the flat, tarred surface of the roof calling out Jazz's name. Then they went around the sides of the building and called down to a man they hoped was there.

"This is ridiculous," Jeremy finally said, putting out a hand and grabbing for Sheraton. "We're not doing any good. He mustn't be here."

"I still think he is," Sheraton said. "Darn it all. I know he's here."

"Well, unless he's posing as a television antenna, I don't know where he could be, Sheraton."

"Jeremy," Sheraton said, stopping his lover from walking to the exit. "I'm not crazy."

"I never said you were. I said you were relentless and would probably be the cause of my nervous breakdown but I never called you crazy."

"I mean, I do hear someone."

"It's your imagination. You *want* to hear someone."

"Listen," Sheraton ordered him. They were quiet for a half a minute but all that Jeremy could hear was the grinding sounds of the cars far below them.

"Sheraton, I-"

"Exactly," Sheraton said with excitement. "Somebody is up here and they're crying."

"Dear Lord." Jeremy blessed himself though he wasn't conscious of doing so. "You might be right."

"I know I am." Sheraton rushed around in such wide, frantic circles as he covered the surface of the roof that Jeremy was afraid that he might fall off though there was a high ledge all around. While he ran, he called to his friend.

"It's coming from here," Sheraton shouted, waving his hand toward a particularly dark section of the roof.

"We already looked there. We did everything but proclaim squatters rights over there."

"Jeremy, I know Jazz is up here and now I'm positive that he's somewhere over there."

Both went, investigated, but still couldn't find Jazz.

"There it goes again," Sheraton said. "I hear it and you do too."

"I hear it but, if it's Jazz, why the bleeding hell isn't he answering us? Does he think we're up here strolling about enjoying the view?"

Soothingly, like a mother to a new born child, Sheraton spoke to Jazz.

"We know you're up here and we want to help you. Honest Jazz, we won't let anyone hurt you. We know you're innocent. Won't you tell us where you are?"

A sob, much louder than the others, rose up to them.

"Where are you, Jazz?" Sheraton was now frenzied.

"Sheraton," Jeremy said. "I think he's down there." He pointed past the partition. "There's a small parapet there. I think it goes in a lot further than we can see from here. I think Jazz is crouched in there."

"He couldn't have gotten down there," Sheraton said, although he was certain that, if anywhere, that would be the spot where they would find Jazz. "Unless... Jeremy, see that statue?"

"It's a saint."

"See that saint," Sheraton corrected himself. "I think that, barefoot, Jazz was able to climb on it and work his way down to that small ledge below."

"If he got down there, let's get him up again."

"Jazz. Are you there?"

A whimper, a direct response to Sheraton's question, came back immediately.

"Jazz," Jeremy sternly said. "Are you there?"

Weak voiced and so faint that they weren't sure if they were hearing it or imaging it, they got a humble yes.

"Come back up here, Jazz," Sheraton said.

"Can't. Scared."

"Oh dear," Sheraton fretted. "He's scared. You go down there and get him, Jeremy."

"He's scared and maybe you think I majored in scaling the sides of building in college? Sheraton, I'm scared too."

"Come on," Sheraton begged. "When we were mugged, you know they bruised my legs badly. I can't do it."

"You want me to stand on the head of a saint? I can be ex-communicated for that."

"Jeremy."

"The things I do for love," Jeremy said, yanking off his shoes and putting one leg over the side of the building. "Better still, the things I do for you."

Far below, Pris stood in one corner of the hospital corridor trying to be as unobtrusive as possible. As she was one of the only ones on the floor who wasn't in uniform-either police officer blue or hospital white-and probably the only person who wasn't rushing around or looking worried, it wasn't quite such an easy feat.

Detective Lawrence, propped up by his associate Detective Stone-went rushing around generously berating hospital staff and condemning his men to hell and back. Pris found that, when she leaned against one of the walls, she could feel the sweat on her back. She stared up at the cracked, dingy white ceiling and wondered what Jeremy and Sheraton were doing now.

Meanwhile, stories above her, a rather scary scene was taking place.

"Look Jazz," Jeremy said, refusing to look down although he couldn't fight the mental image of the street below his feet. "You've got to give me some help here. I'm gay, not a mosquito."

"I don't need help," Jazz said in a flat, lifeless voice. "I don't want anything. Leave me alone."

"You don't really mean that," Sheraton called down, leaning over the side of the building as he held onto Jeremy's shoulders. "It's all going to be OK, Jazz. You have to trust us."

"I don't trust anybody anymore," Jazz sobbed. Now, when he could will his eyes to focus clearly and his brain to clear, Jeremy could see the pathetic figure that Jazz made as he cowered in a bird stained nook. Fortunately for Jeremy, the statue that he was precariously balancing himself on had been adorned with a halo by the sculptor. Whether the saint had earned it or not, it was certainly playing an important safety catch for Jeremy just then.

Jeremy felt as if he were dangling miles about the world although the realization that he could come crashing down to meet it at any moment never left his mind-or his nervous system.

"Jazz, what is all this going to prove?" Jeremy had managed to wangle his way so that now he was standing in front of Jazz. He couldn't see him now-his body had filled in the niche and cut off the light-but he wasn't about to move about just to give Jazz a better view of the western skies.

"They think I killed Gene," Jazz sobbed, stumbling and stuttering each word as if he were a foreigner with a harelip to further hinder his speech. "Maybe I did."

"Maybe?" Jeremy felt like either laughing or shrieking. As he was concentrating too much on holding onto the sides of the cranny he had wedged himself into, he did neither. "Why do you *think* you killed him?"

"They said I did."

"They say many things," Sheraton called down.

As if a certain degree of realization had just struck him, Jazz lifted his head and asked, "Is that Sheraton up there?"

"No," Jeremy said. "It's Jesus. You always heard about how he was coming again and he's come just to see you. Now, let's go up and get you dressed. You wouldn't want to meet him dressed like that, would you?"

"Jeremy." He spoke as if they were the words of a child. Jeremy had a mental image of Jazz sitting on the cold stone sucking his thumb. "I didn't kill him. I don't think I did. They all say I did. They told me that I killed him."

"I'm sure that they did," Jeremy said, testing his agility by releasing his right hand from the decorative scroll around the lip of the niche. He wavered slightly but not enough so that he couldn't quickly catch his balance. "I'm sure they would say anything to scare you."

"Why? I'm just a dumb queen who doesn't hurt anybody."

"That's right. You don't hurt anybody. Remember that, Jazz. Stop screwing up your head. You know you never killed Gene so why not tell that to the police?"

"They say they have proof. Proof that will put me away forever."

"They have proof and you have a mouth. Why didn't you deny everything? Why play the victim? Dressing up is all well and fine if you're into it. Not defending yourself is useless. Don't be a fool."

"Jeremy," Sheraton tentatively whispered. "Maybe this isn't the correct time to antagonize Jazz."

"Antagonize him? Hell and damnation, Sheraton. I'm up here floating hundreds of feet above a concrete sidewalk and you're telling me that maybe I should compliment his complexion instead of trying to talk sense into him?"

"Jazz," Sheraton called. "Come back here with Jeremy. We'll help you. We know things."

"The police know things," Jazz said, crying while he spoke. "They say they know enough to put me away."

Jeremy started to shake his head and then realized how dangerous this was. "Jazz, did you leave your make-up kit at Gene's house?"

"Never," Jazz said firmly. "I never forget to bring my bag of tricks with me. I have it right next to me now." With shaking fingers, Jazz unzipped the soft, lumpy pouch and shoved it near Jeremy's face.

"I'm not sure but that could mean something," Jeremy called up to Sheraton. "Of course, I never thought that when I woke up this morning I'd be hanging on the side of a building looking through an Avon ladies sample kit."

"Jazz," Sheraton said. "You never left any of your cosmetics at Gene's place?"

"Never," Jazz said. In the shadows, Jeremy's eyes were getting accustomed enough to the darkness so that he could see enough to know that Jazz had moved one arm and was now holding something in it. "Do you know how much they charge for some of this stuff?"

"Let's not do any comparative price shopping now," Jeremy recommended. "Let's go somewhere nice and flat and, preferably, below sea level."

"It's not going to matter," Jazz said to him. "They want to put me away. They're going to kill me."

"So, instead of facing up to them and proving yourself, you decided to crawl up here and kill yourself...And me in the bargain. What is wrong with you? The game is far from over."

"They said—"

"Jazz, I don't give a fig what 'they' said. Sheraton is saying many things too. Maybe, instead of playing the coward, you should start using your head to think instead of just using it as a place to park your make-up.

"You didn't kill Gene. You know you're innocent so why not stand up for your rights? Besides, you're not the only one who visited Gene who wore make-up."

"I know," Jazz said, dejected and glum. "He had other women there too. I found their make-up in his bathroom. I questioned him about it but he only started to fight with me."

"This isn't the perfect time for telling me about your domestic squabbles."

"Jazz," Sheraton yelled. "Somebody else left their make-up in Gene's bathroom?"

"Didn't I tell you that before? I found some expensive stuff in there."

"Expensive?" Sheraton's mind went to both Karen and Barbara. The first might not be able to afford expensive cosmetics, the second certainly threw money freely around recently.

"What kind of make-up did you find there?" Sheraton asked.

Jeremy forgot the height, dangled his head back and looked up at Sheraton. "Couldn't we have this discussion someplace else-like on ground level?"

"It was expensive," Jazz repeated. "Also, it was that heavy duty type of base make-up. You know. The type that a woman with acne scarred skin might use."

"Barbara's face is a wreck," Jeremy said quickly. "She spent more time at dermatologists than in class when we were in college."

"You think Barbara left her make-up there?" Jazz sounded confused. "So what?"

Sheraton, disregarding the location of the conference, tossed out a few more questions.

*   *   *

"You still here, pussycat?"

Detective Lawrence sauntered over to Pris with another cup of coffee in his hand. He was dexterous enough to be able to shout and belittle people and drink at the same time.

Pris gave him her best steely look. "I'm concerned about Jazz."

"Jazz isn't your friend. Those other two are."

"He's my friend now," she said. "I have this thing about men who escape from hospital security. I find it a real turn-on."

"Oh yeah?" His smirk was sickening for Pris to see. "I'd like to turn you on just to find out why you're really here. Hey! Where are those two clowns?"

"Two clowns? Did you try the circus?"

"That Baker and the other one," Detective Lawrence shouted. Detective Stone, now standing behind him, gave him the boy's first names.

"Yeah. That's right. Jeremy and Sheraton. Why aren't they here with you?"

"Tonight they're visiting their dear, old Aunt Tilly. It's her night to host the bible meeting."

Detective Stone looked at her. "What are they praying for?"

"That this never becomes a police state."

"Stone," Detective Lawrence shouted. "Put out a bulletin. I think that we've just increased the number of people we're looking for by two. I got a feeling that we're going to find three pussycats tonight."

*   *   *

"Just a little more," Sheraton called out. He was shaking all over but managed to control his nerves so that his muscles were tight and working at their full potential. He disregarded any feelings other than getting Jeremy and Jazz up to safety.

Dangling somewhere between the niche he had just shimmied up from and a few feet of the ledge, Jeremy said: "I guess this isn't the time to tell you I'm afraid of heights."

"Just edge yourself against the side of the building, honey. First you and then we'll get Jazz."

Jazz, using only one hand because he refused to let go of his vanity case, was gripping Jeremy's ankles and tried to hoist him upwards.

"This is crazy," Jeremy gasped as he tried to swing one leg that Jazz had let go of over the side ledge. "We're going to be killed."

"No we're not," Sheraton ordered him. "We're going to have you up here in a second and then we're going to get Jazz. Then, we're going to straighten this whole mess. From what Jazz just told us—"

"Does it really confirm what you suspected when you thought about this last night?" Jazz called out.

"It fits perfectly," Sheraton assured him as he grabbed and tugged at Jeremy's shoulders.

Half rolling and half banging onto the tar papered surface, Jeremy came over the side.

"Now you, Jazz. Help me Jeremy."

"Certainly," Jeremy said, fighting off a wave of dizziness. He refused still to look at how high up he was. "Next time, Jazz, promise me you'll hide out in a basement somewhere."

"There isn't going to be a next time," Sheraton said. "We're going to get Jazz up here, hide him here on the roof and then go and solve this miserable case."

"Gee, that'll be ginger peachy," Jeremy said. "I was afraid I might be able to take a nice, hot bath as you've now yanked my shoulder muscles up to my ears."

Half of Jazz was popped into view. Jeremy grabbed him under his arms while Sheraton wrestled him up by grabbing him around his chest.

"What's that?" Jazz asked, still suspended practically in mid-air. "I hear something."

"It's just my heart," Jeremy said.

"No." Jazz looked at Sheraton. "Somebody is up there with you, aren't they?"

"It's just the two of us," Sheraton told him but, then, a door slammed somewhere and the sounds of heavy, running feet reached him.

"It's all over," Jazz screamed. "Let me go. Let me fall. I don't want to have to deal with the police again. Please. Tell them I confessed. Tell them anything. Just don't let them touch me again."

"Jazz, stop wriggling like that," Sheraton ordered him. "You're almost here."

Shaking and trying to work himself loose from their grasps, Jazz laughed hysterically.

"I don't want to have to go back to jail. Let me fall. I want to die. Let me die. Please."

"Dear God," Sheraton cried to Jeremy. "Hold onto him. I can't. I can't hold him."

"What the hell is going on up here?" A voice shouted at them as a flashlight shone in their eyes, blinding them.

A yell, piercing and awful, broke the night.

ELEVEN

"Pussycats. I don't think you know how much trouble you're in right now."

Jeremy, cold and feeling the aftermath shock effects of his adventure, was in no mood for the man.

"If the police had bothered to even try to do their job-"

"Keep it up," he said, in a school masterly way. The only thing missing was a note book and a pencil for him to jot down all the blasphemy and record the sins. "You've got a lot of explaining to do."

It would have been impossible to get into the tight corner that Detective Stone and Detective Lawrence had backed Jeremy and Sheraton into. They surrounded them like a wall of invincible flesh and hatred. Pris was bobbing around behind the detectives as close to the uncharmed circle as possible but she couldn't break through. She could, still, hear every word and every threat rather clearly.

"What happened?" a breathless voice demanded as an arm grabbed Pris from behind and almost knocked the purse out of her hands.

Pris whirled around to face a pale faced Marty and the speaker- his wife Karen.

Karen was dressed in cranberry colored stretch pants and a shapeless blouse that had some motif of a revolutionary war print on it done up in bright, cheery shades of red and green. Pris was glad that wars were fought so that Karen could have a blouse made to record the historical event.

"Jazz escaped from his hospital room," Pris said, wondering how they seemed to be the only two people in the world who hadn't heard the news.

The florescent light made both of them look a sickly pea green color.

"You mean he got away?" Marty seemed relieved more than anything else. "The police can't find him?"

"Sheraton and Jeremy found Jazz."

"Damn them to hell and back," Karen sputtered. She yanked off a sleeveless vest as a boxer would doff a robe before a big fight. "Who the hell do they think they are? Can't they stay out of anything?"

"They think they're friends of Jazz," Pris curtly told the other woman. "While the rest of you were busy dry cleaning your leisure suits-or whatever the bloody hell one does with a leisure suit-they were trying to help a friend-*your* friend."

"My wife is upset," Marty apologized, speaking over and beyond his wife's cold glare.

"And where is the rediscovered Jazz now?" Karen snapped.

"I don't know," Pris admitted, suddenly remembering how confused and how much in the dark she really was.

Detective Lawrence had his men march Jeremy and Sheraton down to the front reception desk but nowhere could she see Jazz.

"Karen," Sheraton called out, standing on his toes and peering over Detective Lawrence's shoulders. "We have to speak to you."

"Pussycat," the man said, half turning to look at the couple and then turning back as if to disregard them totally. "You have to speak to me and only to me. You can have a nice, long gossip with your friends when you get out of court."

"Out of court?" Pris found the words gave her a sudden burst of strength. Enough strength so that she broke between the two men and began shouting at them.

"They've been doing all the work around here," Pris said, waving her fingers dangerously close to the man's chin. "It was your man who let Jazz escape."

"And it was your friends who obstructed justice and hampered the work of the department," Detective Stone recited.

"What is going on here?" Karen impatiently asked. "We dropped by to visit a friend and we walk into the middle of what looks like a police lounge."

Sheraton, never daunted-not even now under extenuating cir-cumstances-stepped closer to Karen.

"We have to talk. About make-up."

Absently, Karen put one hand up to her face. "Make up? You want to talk about beauty tips now?"

"You heard your friend," Detective Lawrence said, nodding his head toward Pris. "These two are doing all the work for us. Why, I can't tell you how long we've procrastinated down at the squad room about asking those important questions-like how to highlight the apples of your cheeks."

"Did Gene wear make-up?" Sheraton asked, ignoring the detec-tives and speaking solely to Karen.

"Why, how should I know?" She retreated behind her husband as she generally did when confronted with something she didn't want to handle.

"Karen. You were there. You might have noticed if Gene had any cosmetics lying around the place."

"Marty was there too," she said, pushing her husband so that he almost tripped due to the force of her shove. "Why not ask him?"

"Because you would notice something like that. A woman gener-ally would."

Her eyes strained themselves into small slits.

"Are you trying to say that Gene was into drag like Jazz?"

"Having make-up hanging around a man's house doesn't mean he actually wears it," Jeremy said. "Somebody could have left it there."

"Then, if there was any make-up in his bathroom, you already know how it got there. Jazz left it there." Karen seemed so pleased with herself now that it was several seconds after Sheraton said, "We never said he had make-up in his bathroom. You did, Karen." that she realized her mistake.

"I noticed a jar of some crap on his shelf in the bathroom when I was there once," Karen hesitantly said. She was thinking out the way to tell the story as she spoke. "Marty was there that night though I'm sure he won't remember.

"I asked Gene about it. Actually, I kidded him about it. At the time, I thought he might have had a girl friend staying over with him from time to time."

"Gene didn't have girl friends staying over," Sheraton said. "You know that, Karen."

"Whether they spent the night there or not, I had no way of knowing." She tossed her head back defiantly. "He just said that someone had left it there and, later, he said to me that he never threw it out because Jazz used it once or twice."

"Jazz?"

"That's what he said," Karen shouted. The room, still quelled with officers but thinning out now that most of the problem was solved. No one seemed to be making any sort of effort to discover what was happening besides Jeremy and Sheraton.

"Did he say that Jazz used the stuff or that people used it?" Jeremy concentrated his words hoping that the importance of the question wouldn't be lost on Karen.

"I don't remember. I didn't have a court stenographer with me at the time."

Sheraton, gingerly putting his hand on Karen's shoulder, asked: "Did you ever use any of the base cream that you found in Gene's bathroom?"

"I tried it," she admitted. "It was real expensive stuff. I didn't much like it. Fortunately, I don't need to wear *that* much make-up."

"What do you mean?"

"It was real heavy duty crap. Much too heavy for the pores of your skin to breathe once you had it on."

"A real cover-up type of make-up then?"

She nodded at Sheraton and seemed relieved. "That's why I knew it had to be Jazz's. Only a man, or a very hirsute woman, would have to put that sort of stuff on their face."

"It could also have been used by a woman with acne scars," Pris said.

Detective Stone seemed ready to snap. "So, all we have to look for are drag queens and women who don't buy depilatories or Clearasil.

Pris said, "We're trying to narrow down the list, not widen the circle."

"If you'd be quiet for just a minute and let us explain something, you might have the list narrowed down right to the killer you're so eagerly looking for," Jeremy shouted, causing another flock of nurses to shake their heads.

"Pussycat," Detective Lawrence said. "You've got five minutes. Start talking."

*　　　*　　　*

"You don't have to come with us," Jeremy said, turning to Pris.

A totally blank look of confusion and hurt swelled up over her facial features.

"I want to, Jeremy."

"It's not going to be fun," he warned.

Pris pulled herself out of the cab and reached herself up to her full height. She had a certain limber way of stretching her body up so that she appeared to tower over him now.

"Let's get a few things straight, Baker. I'm your friend. I also happen to be a woman.

"If nothing else, haven't we learned enough about the dangers of stereotyping? If you still think that dyke's are ballsy, gutsy women then you're a fool. If you think a woman still faints dead away at the first sign of a garter snake, you're even more of a fool.

"I don't like being weak and I don't like what is about to happen."

"Then why bother?" Jeremy asked, paying the cab driver and wondering what he was making of this.

"Because," Sheraton interrupted. "Pris is a friend. Friends do stick together."

"No matter how weird your old buddies may be, it happens to be true," Pris told Jeremy. "Friends-real friends-stick together at a time like this."

Jeremy stared at the building looming in front of him. Mentally, he counted the stories until he got to the floor where he wanted to be then. The lights were on though he could see no shadows cast on the yellowed window shades.

"Then, come on," he said in way of an apology. "I have a feeling we're going to need all the friends we can get from now on."

*   *   *

Barbara, wearing a slinky, flowing gown of silver Lame, answered the bell on the first ring.

"What do you want?" she asked, waving a crystal stemmed martini glass dangerously close to their faces.

Inside, the apartment seemed done up in nothing else but overly plush carpeting that was long, fuzzy and unreasonably furry.

Sheraton recollected seeing a picture of Jayne Mansfield's bathroom once and this room seemed to have been decorated in the same demented way.

Peering deep within the sea shell pink apartment, Jeremy asked: "May we enter?"

"I'm not really up to social calls," she sniffed, refusing to move from her guard post position at the door. Languidly she leaned against the door frame and struck a pose that was both preposterous and funny to see. "It's late and I'm very tired."

"Funny," Sheraton said, swinging his lithe body under her arm and entering the apartment via that route. "I think that you would be ready for company at any hour."

About a yard and a half of dangling bracelets of silver lashed out trying to catch Sheraton as he marched in.

"How dare you," she hissed, tossing her hair. back but keeping a curtain of it carefully positioned over one half of her face. "I'll have you arrested for trespassing. All of you."

"Going to call up your friends at the police force?" Jeremy asked, reaching for a pink, slim lined phone and handing it to her. "You are the police officers benevolent association in person, aren't you?"

"I have certain friends," she said, grabbing the phone but only putting it down on a white, low slung table. "Now, get out of here."

"We went to the hospital this evening to see Jazz," Sheraton said. "Aren't you the least bit curious as to what happened there?"

"No." Her face said otherwise.

"He ran up to the roof," Jeremy said. "We tried to rescue him."

"Tried to rescue him? He's dead?" A certain faded type of triumph filled her voice. "I can't say as I'm sorry."

Jeremy told her, "Why all the rejoicing, Barbara? Do you think that Jazz flung himself off the side of a building without first telling us a few things?"

"Things?" She emptied the drink into her mouth and looked as if she were about to spit it out. "I really don't care. The man was crazy."

"He had a lot to say about Gene," Sheraton hinted, running his fingers over a sand colored recliner. "Aren't you curious?"

Barbara rushed about the apartment. Her negligee flapped freely with her long strides. She snapped off an elaborate stereo system that was playing some punk sounding music.

"I don't give a damn about Jazz or any man. He's dead. Now get out of here."

"OK," Sheraton said, giving an obvious signal to Jeremy and Pris and heading toward the door. "Of course, we aren't the only one's who heard Jazz's confession."

"So?" Barbara seemed slightly mollified. "Little Miss Bull Dyke here was with you. What do I care?"

"Pris was downstairs and missed all the fun," Jeremy told Barbara. "It was a few of your favorite tricks who heard the less-than-entertaining story that Jazz had to tell. Oh, by the way, they love what you can do with a banana. Learn how to do it with a watermelon and I may ask to have it put on a web site."

"What do you bloody fools think? Do you believe that I'm going to turn into an hysterical woman and tell you how I killed Gene?" Barbara tossed her head back, laughed and then threw the empty glass off the table with her foot. "I'm not a fool."

"You're not a fool," Pris said. "If half the stories we heard about you tonight are true, you might be double jointed though."

"Look, this is my home. Mine. I don't need to hear these insults against my character. I have rights, you know!"

"You really were friendly with Gene, weren't you?" Jeremy asked.

"I told you that," she dryly responded. "You were the one who refused to believe it."

"You told us that Gene was after you. It was the other way around, wasn't it?"

"It was love," Barbara said, walking over to a stainless steel bar set up in one corner of the room and pouring herself a fresh drink. "Who remembers who chased who?"

"Gene was probably not very flattered that a woman would make such an obvious play for him," Sheraton said. "He didn't respond or return the affection. It did come in handy, I might imagine, when people like Alan or Mitch dropped by. Having a woman throw herself at him was just what he needed to complete the ego trip he was always on."

Barbara snapped, "You didn't even have the decency to pick up a phone and call him occasionally. How the hell can you stand there and analyze a man you didn't know?"

"It's so classic it's pathetic," Sheraton said. "A man who's asexual feels a lot of pressure from his peers. Why isn't he dating a woman? Is he gay? Gene couldn't stand the thought of that, could he? So, he finds something better that temporarily ends the speculation on his sexual interests. He finds a woman who flings herself all over him but doesn't actually demand sex from him. It's all a game. She's his devoted love slave but only in public. When there's an audience about, she puts on a love-starved routine for them with Gene playing the idolized one."

"If that's true, then how come Karen and Marty didn't know about me?"

"Because," Sheraton continued, "you only put on the act for a rather selected audience, didn't you? Jazz was one of your favorites."

"So we're back to Jazz, are we?" She studied her fingernails. They were long, filed to a razor sharpness and painted in shiny silver to match the robe. "Then, Jazz got jealous. He wanted to be me. He wanted to have Gene enjoy his attention the way Gene enjoyed all the attention I lavished upon him.

"I didn't tell you that Gene rejected me because it hurt my pride. No woman could stand rejection from a man. If you know a woman," she said, eyeing Pris distastefully, "then ask her. She'll tell you the same thing."

"You put the act on for Jazz," Jeremy said. "That much is true. Who else was privy to these SRO performances of yours?"

"Perhaps, Jeremy dear, you send out invitations when you feel horny and you want to get your rocks off. I don't."

"You loved Gene so much that you idolized him," Sheraton said. "Yet, you didn't know about the drugs."

"A woman always refuses to see what she doesn't want to see. Especially a woman in love."

"First off," Jeremy commanded. "Let's cut the 'love' crap, Barbara. You didn't love Gene any more than I love you. He was the perfect patsy for you and your drug operation."

"Oh? So now I'm the drug pusher, am I?" She walked around her apartment, tottering on high heels that she obviously wasn't use to wearing. "Does this look like an opium den to you?"

"It looks like the perfect whore's fantasy place but that isn't the point. You hooked Gene on drugs and then told him that if he wanted to have his supply of candy, he had to start pushing the stuff as well as just smoking it. You didn't care how he sold it or how many agents he assigned to push the shit, just so long as he made the sales to keep you in pengoir sets."

"My, don't I come off in this little fantasy piece of yours as the perfect bitch?"

Sheraton said, "I imagine having friends on the police force made it easier for you."

Bitterly, she avoided making eye contact as she said, "Yeah. They just love to see me sitting on their desks, licking an ice cream cone every time I get lost."

"Gene was so far gone," Sheraton continued, "that he couldn't get out of the deal he made with you. He had to have the drugs and you forced him to sell the stuff....Amongst other things."

Barbara seemed to have been enjoying most of what Sheraton and Jeremy had to say until then. Sharply, she swung around and screamed: "Now what the hell are you saying?"

"You supplied the drugs to Gene. Who supplied them to you?"

"I assure you," she said in an exaggerated drawl, "that I don't know what you're talking about, honey."

"The police found your cover up, base make-up in Gene's bathroom," Sheraton told her. "They found some of it under Gene's fingernails. They stopped there. They didn't examine the stuff they found in the bathroom. What do you think is going to happen to you when they do?"

"Why, I don't know what you mean." A certain frenzied look washed over her. Barbara wasn't as confident now.

"Jazz used some of your base foundation make-up," Sheraton said. "But he wasn't using it the night Gene died. He came to our place. We saw his face. We saw the freckles. He has a very light beard and doesn't need that stuff."

"And you're saying I have a beard?" she asked, stroking her weak, hairless jaw.

"How about other hair follicles that the police found mixed in with the make-up under Gene's nails?" Sheraton asked. "How about loose skin cells and so on which they also are examining right now? Do you know what that will tell them?"

"I only used that stuff once or twice," Barbara screamed. "I still have those damn scars from when I had teen age acne. I get paranoid over it. That's why I left the jar in Gene's bathroom. I bought it, used it once, but didn't use it after that."

"Somebody else used the stuff," Sheraton said. "However, it's your fingerprints on the jar. You're going to have a lot of explaining to do."

"That's crazy," Barbara gasped, flinging the remainder of her drink into a small sink built into the bar. "They won't hassle me."

"They will now," Jeremy promised her. "We're making them. Raise enough of a stink and you can get anything you want."

"You bastard," she cried. "Do you know what you're doing?"

Jeremy grimly nodded. "Yes, Barbara. We're forcing you to name and identify Mr. Big."

A woman stepped out of Barbara's bedroom dressed almost identical to Barbara.

"That's Ms. Big."

*   *   *

Pris stared straight ahead and found herself suddenly succumbed into a gentle nightmare world.

All around, soft lights and even softer music drifted throughout the room. The windows and most of the walls were covered from ceiling to floor with long, billowy fine mesh drapes in subtle shades of pink and coral white. Her feet were mired in the deep, shag carpeting that seemed-at times-to be rising up at her feet and swallowing them as if the pile were actually crimson colored wisps of smoky fog. It was all a set from an art decoish movie and somehow she, Jeremy and Sheraton had gotten confused enough to stumble in the middle of it.

"You shouldn't be here," Barbara said in a coolly relaxed voice to the newcomer.

Sheraton and Jeremy knew what they had expected but now, actually seeing it in front of them, it seemed too preposterous to accept.

Standing amidst the draperies, in a long, wheat colored caftan, was Mitch. His face was heavy with cosmetic cover ups and his eyes were heavily outlined and accentuated in a mock Cleopatra style. It looked, for the initial moment of shock, as if Barbara had dressed up a doll and was parading it about for them.

"How much of your story have you actually told the police," a soft voiced Mitch asked them. He suddenly had transformed himself from a loud-mouthed creature into a demure debutante. Gone was the street smarmy ways only to be replaced by an imaginativeness of what a woman might be.

"Mitch," Barbara said, speaking giddily as if she had been caught playing the part of the fool. "Go inside. I can handle this."

"Can you, dear?" Mitch ran a hand through the deep black wig he had on; fingers flitting through tight masses of upswept curls only to stop at a pearl crusted barrette. "Can you handle anything properly? I doubt it. Look at the mess you've made of everything so far."

"How long had you been in love with Gene?" Jeremy asked, prompted on by the disbelief because none of this could truly be happening.

"Probably for as long as he rejected me," Mitch said in mincing, choppy tones as if he were speaking words that didn't mean anything but were rather effective for the performance expected of him. "Isn't that always the way, darlings? We never want what we can have."

"Gene, from what I've heard, had a thing against love," Pris said, wishing that Barbara would offer her a generous slug from the martini pitcher sitting on top of the bar. "Gay, straight or whatever. Especially drag."

"Gene didn't know what was good for him," Mitch said, leaning against a slipper styled sofa and letting his painted nails dig deeply into the salmon colored satin fabric covering it. "He had nothing in his life. He was argumentative, foul tempered and a silly fool."

"And that's why you loved him so?" Jeremy asked.

"That's what I consider the ultimate challenge," Mitch smiled. "He rejected lovers-especially homosexual ones-so he was a challenge that I had to accept.

"I always had a thing for fancy clothes and pretty finery," he continued, petting his caftan as he spoke. Wisps of marabou ballet stepped down to the rug. "Of course, Gene didn't know what was good for him. When he lost his job, I selected a way to help him…And myself, of course."

"You were pushing drugs and you decided to make Gene the CEO of your operation."

"No, Jeremy. I decided to help the poor boy. I offered him some pot-a harmless trifle these days-and he took to it immediately. I noticed the change instantly. He was less intense and a lot less up tight about everything."

Sheraton shook his head as Mitch spoke. "You make it sound more like an endowment for his good. Can't you see what it made him become, Mitch?"

"I couldn't help it if Gene had the personality of an addict. He enjoyed doing drugs. It allowed him, or so he felt, to be able to speak freely and to say whatever he wanted to say."

"In other words," Sheraton clarified, "Gene could get as angry and as abusive as he wanted to get. He could blame it on the drugs speaking."

"Exactly," Mitch cried, clapping his hands together childishly. "He did so have a filthy temper, you know. Of course, he was smart enough not to use it on me."

"Of course he wouldn't," Sheraton said. "He knew that you were the one who was giving him the drugs free of charge-at first."

"I couldn't be the patron saint for the perpetually stoned forever. He had to reciprocate in some way."

"And you decided that sex would be the perfect form of payment," Jeremy said angrily. "The only trouble is, Gene didn't want to be touched by anyone. That must have made you quite angry."

"It hurt," Mitch decided to say. "But then, I'm a resourceful gal. He wanted the drugs and there was a price to pay for them. I believe that's what's known as enterprise."

In disbelief, Jeremy said: "There are a few terms for it but enterprise isn't one of them."

"Jeremy. Must you always be so gruff? You must be an absolute tiger in the bedroom."

"Mitch," Barbara husked. "Do you have to tell them all this?"

"But dear," Mitch cooed. "It doesn't matter. Who will believe them?

"Now. As I was saying. Gene wouldn't give me a fair payment for all the goodies I supplied him with so, he had to make some contribution. That's when I decided to make him sell some drugs. I honestly didn't think that he would. I mean, I figured he would try it, get scared like the little boy he actually was, and then forget the whole thing. How was I to know that he had such a calculating mind?"

"Gene wasn't quite as sweet as you'd like to make him out to have been," Sheraton said directly. "By all accounts, he had a nasty streak. When did he start to use it against you?"

"He never could appreciate anything," Mitch pined. "I certainly didn't want the likes of Karen selling my goodies. Why, if she knew who the source was, she'd demand a bigger cut for herself and that wouldn't do."

Jeremy coughed. "I would suppose that's when Barbara made her grand re-entrance into Gene's life?"

"Yes," Mitch agreed, seemingly pleased by the accuracy of the guess. "Barbara, of course, is a trusted friend-of mine! Gene didn't know that. She had to report to me about just what he was up to when I wasn't around to monitor him.

"Gene didn't want her in his life but, as I pointed out to him, she could be another of his agents. Also, I broadly hinted about all the rumors that were flying about Gene's sexual identity. I let it slip that Barbara wasn't interested in Gene-in that way-but if he were to slip her some grass or coke, she would reciprocate by posing as his love. Gene's gifts to Barbara came right back to me so there was no loss of profits."

"Gene went for this idea?" Sheraton asked Mitch.

"Not at first," he said. "He squawked but he knew I had him where I wanted him-well, not exactly where I wanted him but someplace where he couldn't kick up too much of a fuss. Then, fate intervened in the form of Karen. Somehow, she got the hots for Gene and he had to use some excuse to keep her away."

"I suggested a bayonet," Barbara said loudly.

"I," Mitch smiled, "suggested that he simply let it be known about Barbara being his love interest. Karen didn't tell you that she knew about Barbara because she couldn't stand to think that any man would prefer Barbara to her.

"I must say, I admired Gene so. He was able to manipulate Karen and got her to do his dirty work for him all with just a promise or two casually dropped."

"How *casually* were those promises dropped," Sheraton asked. "I think that Gene played games with people. I think that he came onto them."

"He learned a lot from me. He learned how to pretend and to act as if he was interested in somebody. He used it on Karen and-sex starved hag that she is-she fell for it."

Verbally, Jeremy played out the scene for Mitch. "He would do things like sweet talk Karen. Perhaps he managed to have his shirt off or his pants undone when she knocked on the door?"

"He was so shy about nudity," Mitch said, with what looked like an actual blush rising up but barely visible under the heavy pancake make-up. "I taught him about the art of illusion. A flash of under-pants, a flexed muscle, a sly reference to the size of his manhood. Wet the appetite and feed the imagination. It's all a game."

"It's all a game," Jeremy mimicked. "How did you feel about the game when he started playing it on you?"

"I was hurt," a shy voiced Mitch admitted. "I was truly surprised when he started play acting for me. Didn't he know that he couldn't fool the teacher?"

"But that wasn't why you eventually killed Gene," Sheraton calmly said. "You didn't know half the things that Gene was up to, did you? You didn't find out about his black mailing schemes. Especially his plans for Marty." '

A look of sheer anger shot through Mitch. He lost the theatrical pose and stood up in a very unfeminine way.

"Marty was a fool. Gene wasn't pulling in his share. He had to start paying me for the grass and the coke I was slipping to him. He was smoking and snorting more of it than he was selling. I'm not a non-profit organization. I had to be firm with him. I told him that he had to start pulling in the money or the candy would stop coming to him. That was when he hit upon the plan of blackmailing Marty.

"Marty is a schmuck. He's too good to be believed. Gene knew it. I didn't know that Gene would have the balls to approach Marty-especially when Marty's wife was hanging around Gene's apartment every day she wasn't playing bridge. But, as you already said, he had a nasty streak and he wasn't afraid to let it rule his actions.

"He got hold of some fancy camera-the type that doesn't need a flash. He followed Marty to a bar near where he worked—"

"And he got some pictures of Marty having a drink with some gay buddies of his," Sheraton said. "And, he got a good shot of you dressed up in drag."

Mitch sat on the low sofa, allowed the caftan to part and exposed nylon stockinged legs that were surprisingly shapely.

"Gene got carried away with his blackmailing plans. He only intended to use the information to get dough out of Marty: once he saw my picture, he decided to go and double the sweepstakes winnings.

"He knew about this," Mitch said, dropping his hands from the top of his wig down to his toes that were exposed in sandals. "I didn't play it up much but, he knew. After he had the pictures developed, he decided to play games with me again. This time, he pretended to be very interested in drag. He used Jazz as an example. He had him hanging around-to sell drugs-and he told me how fascinated he was by the whole thing.

"Love struck fool that I was, I believed him. He played up to it and I loved it. I loved it until I realized what he had in store for me."

"He was going to blackmail Marty for money and he was planning on blackmailing you for free drugs," Sheraton guessed aloud.

"He did it right out of a B movie," Mitch complained, much as one would fret over a hang nail. "He did the whole seduction number for me. He stood dressed in those tacky jeans and flannel shirts he always wore. He had me go into his bathroom and do myself up properly. The first time he played that game with me, I was in pig heaven-if you'll pardon the expression. I didn't even realize that I hadn't even gotten a slap and a tickle from the man."

"What did you get then?"

"I got stuck in one of the oldest scams going. Gene had that camera set up on some sort of timer system. He had it hidden—"

"Hidden in the cabinet where he kept the breakfast cereals," Sheraton cried. It had to be; hadn't the police commented on how it had been ransacked?

"I didn't know it…The first time I didn't know about it. I don't honestly know what he was going to do with those pictures but I didn't get to be where I am today by being a jackass."

"Mitch," Barbara complained. "You're telling them too much."

"Dear," Mitch said, rubbing his tongue over his lips. "I've told them nothing. Gene took some supposedly incriminating pictures of me. He tried it again. I heard the camera going off. The metal of that cabinet seemed to intensify the sound. He had a little hole drilled for the lens. I could hear the timer going off and the shutter tripping.

"The first time he tried it, I let him get away with it. I thought that he just wanted pictures to look at when he was alone. You know what I mean; something to excite the boy. The second time, I wasn't in the mood.

"He had it all so romantic. Soft lights-so flattering for a lady-and he was rather affectionate. Nothing serious, mind you. It was all Sunday school stuff. I waited patiently for him to make his move but, alas, he didn't. He even did a semi-strip tease for me. It was cute but I wanted something more."

"He got down to his underwear," Sheraton said. "You responded and he stopped you."

Mitch looked up in surprise. "Have you had the same thing happen to you, Sheraton?"

Despite Barbara's near-frantic protests, Mitch continued as if spellbound by his own story.

"Yes. He had this look-but-don't-touch idea. I played along with it for a while but then I was fed up with the stupidity of it all. I told him I knew about the camera. That's when he got nasty.

"He didn't even bother to put his pants back on; he just started shouting at me. The names he called me! He threatened me."

"And you killed him," Pris said with difficulty. Her throat felt as if it had closed on her.

"Dear. *You* might always hurt the one you love but I certainly don't.

"I did take that silly camera out of it's hiding place and even had to defend myself against Gene's quite violent attack on me but that was all I did."

"See," Barbara said, sounding as abrasive as usual. "Now, why don't you all go home. You've had your fun for the night."

"You didn't kill Gene?" Sheraton asked Mitch.

"Not I," Mitch said. "Forgive the Cliché but, I make love and not war."

"So, then it had to be Barbara," Sheraton simply said. "Your cohort in crime."

"Now do you see what you've done?" Barbara screamed.

"Dear Barbara," Mitch giggled. "They're just sucking wind-and I can assure you that they've probably sucked a lot worse."

"It was Barbara's make-up in Gene's bathroom," Sheraton pointed out. "Besides Mitch, you weren't the only woman scorned by Gene. So, if it wasn't you, that leaves Barbara."

"As we've already informed the police," Jeremy said.

"You bastards," Barbara hollered wildly. She got red in the face and began to move like a hunted animal. "Damn you, Mitch. I didn't kill him. You did."

"The poor girl is obviously on the verge of yet another of her famous break-downs," Mitch yawned. "It does get tiresome after awhile. How is it that some women can never enjoy the gift of their sex?"

"You think you have me cornered," Barbara shouted. "You think I'm going to go to prison so that you can run around looking like a Clown College drop-out? Well, let me tell you something, buddy boy. I didn't destroy those negatives. I have my security. You try to pin that death on me and I'll screw you."

"You kept the negatives?" Mitch sounded mildly amused. "How quaint." He seductively ran a finger beneath the caftan. When he pulled it out, a small, nickel plated pistol was attached to it.

"Where are they, bitch?"

"I'm not giving them to you," Barbara screamed. She was standing flush to the door so Sheraton, Jeremy and Pris knew they were trapped. "You killed him. I was there. You think I'm going to get locked away for something you did?"

"You shan't get locked away," Mitch sighed, still holding the gun. "It was all your idea in the first place. Everything. You even were stupid enough to drop some drugs in Jeremy and Sheraton's apartment the night we went there to firm up our alibi's."

"By the way," Jeremy asked. "Which of you was Snoopy and which was Mickey?"

"You even knew that?" Mitch seemed pleased. "It was only a gentle, love tap you received. You see, Marty and Karen couldn't talk to the police. They had too much at stake. Jazz, poor dear, was too stupid to say anything relevant. Alan…Well, Alan can be handled. He has quite a drug dependency. How fortunate that he found me.

"Only you and Sheraton couldn't be easily manipulated so, Barbara came up the wild idea of scaring you into submission."

The fear of Mitch's gun plainly in sight made even Sheraton grow giddy. He said, "Still wondering if it worked or not?"

"It really doesn't matter now," Mitch said. "I have too much to lose if Barbara is going to tell the police that I killed Gene. The shame of having it announced that I was caught up in a crime of passion is too much for me to bear. So, I know that you've been generous enough to tell the police that Barbara killed Gene-and Jazz can't protest the point-I shall just have to arrange it so that she can't speak the truth. In fact, I shall make it look like a cross fire. Four more deaths. Messy but, unfortunately, necessary."

"Don't let him kill me," Barbara cried. "He killed Gene. He killed once and he'll kill again."

"I had to kill him," Mitch said, rising up. "I didn't want to kill him-he amused me so. You, however, do not amuse me. You overplayed your part and you made it come to this.

"No, dear Barbara. You and the rest of them have to go."

Barbara stood thunder struck still in front of the door. Suddenly, the door caved in and she was knocked down by the blow and partially crushed as the door fell on top of her.

Jeremy grabbed Pris and Sheraton and they half-ducked and half-flew into a corner of the room.

"Pussycat," Detective Lawrence screamed at Mitch, "you have the right to remain silent—"

That was all he said as a burst of gun fire buzzed out of Mitch's pistol.

Epilogue

It took some time, and a decided one at that, for the results to reach Jeremy and Sheraton. The others, Karen and Marty especially, seemed to have lost enough interest in the whole matter that it proved senseless to inform them of the thin trickling of information that they finally received.

Jazz, no where near dead but merely startled and in need of sedation, had pulled through the worst of his nightmare with a shrug of his padded shoulders. That surprised Sheraton but, then, so did many things these days.

Walking along the Morton Street pier, Jeremy was unusually quiet. Sheraton had tried to get his lover to open up, explore the feelings. It was useless.

"How are you handling all this?" Jeremy asked, tossing a grease stained pop corn bag into an overflowing wire basket.

The cold, salty wind thrashed through Sheraton's hair but he hardly noticed.

"I feel confused at times. Also hurt. Most of all, I'm surprised."

"You really thought you knew our friends, didn't you?"

A rough, splintery post was vacant and Sheraton sat gently on it as he spoke.

"I suppose we all have that secret side of us that we don't want others to know about. Still, it's just the shock of quite so many revelations hitting us at once. Gene was into drugs, blackmailing and who knows what else. Marty and Karen were suppose to have a stable, solid marriage despite it all."

"I notice you've taken to omitting Mitch and Barbara from your talks," Jeremy smiled, digging a stuck kernel out from between his teeth. If he wanted to be symbolic about everything, that popcorn would be a perfect piece of illustrated typification to use.

"Didn't you once say, 'No surprise means no pain'? I guess I wasn't quite as surprised at the nature of their characters."

"It was all the other stuff that's blown you for one of your country miles, eh?"

"Jeremy, have we changed too?"

"Only for the better."

"I thought I knew people," Sheraton moaned, his head flagging about as if the wind were about to detach it at any minute. "I don't know them at all."

"You knew them a heck of a lot better than the police detectives did and they're trained for that sort of thing.

"Detective Lawrence still can't understand how he failed so miserably while you, pussycat, had Jazz's nature down flat. He would have crucified him if it hadn't been for you."

"For us."

Jeremy felt angry and stern but he still managed to involuntarily falling into a smile.

"I was pretty damn heroic, wasn't I?"

"You also solved the whole case," Sheraton reminded him. "You were the one who noticed the make-up on Mitch's face the night we met him over on Christopher Street."

"I recall thinking that he hadn't washed himself."

"And that was the clue that was shown to us but hidden," Sheraton said. "He couldn't wipe off that heavy make-up Barbara bought. Not well enough so that a trace or two didn't stay on his skin.

"Neither he or Barbara are actually killers at heart. It was not premeditated. It was just an act of frustration on Mitch's part-or so some smart attorney is going to say when they try to get him off."

"Any attorney will get Mitch off a lot quicker if they cop a plea of insanity."

"For years we wrote Mitch off as just a pest so we never considered him seriously," Sheraton said into the wind. A spray, fine and filled with brine, washed over his face. He wished it would wash over his spirits and rejuvenate them.

Sitting down beside him, Jeremy did the unimaginable-he put an arm around Sheraton in public.

"We haven't lost friends," he said. "We gained one. Pris is a pretty important person to have around and I think we're going to know her for quite some time."

"I'm glad about that," Sheraton said, enjoying the display of affection he was receiving. "And, she is one heck of a lady. When that gun of Mitch's went off, I was scared silly. She didn't blink an eye."

"Luckily Mitch's aim was as rotten as his personality," Jeremy sighed. "Or else, he might have hit Detective Lawrence and you know how I'd hate to have anything to have happened to him."

"He was only doing his job," Sheraton said softly. "Just like, in an odd sort of way, I was only doing my job.

"Did I ever thank you?"

"For what?"

Grinning madly as the wind picked up in intensity, Sheraton answered: "For allowing me to get it out of my system. It was important to me. I had to find out what happened to Gene and why he was killed. Today, now, I'm not sure why."

"Because you're a person who has to do things like that just like I'm the guy who's always going to bitch and complain about it."

"But, you came through like a trooper."

"We both came through it together," Jeremy said, loosening his grip on Sheraton and standing. "I guess that it will teach me never to feel bored again. I don't think I can stand that much excitement."

"It's going to happen again," Sheraton prophesied. "Maybe not murder but there's a big world out there that we don't know anything about yet. I guess it's time we started. Is it time yet for us to finally grow up?"

" 'There must be a way out of this crazy game we play out to the end'," Jeremy quoted.

"I know that," Sheraton said, brushing himself off as he followed Jeremy back home. "That's from one of Gordon Lightfoot albums."

"So. You do listen to them."

Sheraton was honestly surprised that Jeremy hadn't known that he had been listening, and probably always would be. "With the volume level that you play them at, the entire postal code district we live in must hear them.

"I also know the next line. 'Take away the in-between and think about the good things now and then.'"

"Speaking of good things," Jeremy said in a low growl. "How about heading home?"

"Good movie on Home Box Office you want to catch?"

"I've got what I want to catch," Jeremy said, taking Sheraton's arm and heading home.